Big Blue Nation
by:
Amy Leigh McCorkle

mailto:AlMccorkle6875@aol.com

ISBN # 978-0-6151-5129-8

for everyone who has ever dared
to dream

&

for MaMaw, the original
storyteller

Chapter One

Adam Paul Matthews knew a hot story when he smelled one. Only thing was, he hadn't smelled a hot story in almost three years. Being a freelance sports journalist in the Big Blue Nation was the best job in th biz, but it was the most cutthroat. Hell, there had really only been two coaches who had thrived in the system and their successors had been chewed up and spit out by it. One by a scandal that had rocked the big blue University of Kentucky Wildcats. And even though the other two coaches had brought home one national championship a piece they could not hold a candle to the house that Rupp built and one that Pitino had saved. Basketball had not been fun under their tenure. Not that they were bad coaches. They just weren't made for UK ball. The Big Blue Nation wanted their ticket punched for the Final Four every year. They wanted conference championships as bad as they wanted national ones. And a top twenty ranking-at least during the regular season. It was a demanding job. It was a blistering job. But with the right coach it could be a match made in heaven. UK was the premiere coaching job in the NCAA. And now that Tubby had left for a college whose biggest money making sport was wrestling the position was open.

Names were being tossed around, Billy Gillispe, Tom Izzo, Tom Crean, but Adam knew what the Big Blue Nation wanted. Everyone knew what this nation wanted. They wanted Nick Ruiz of the Florida Gators and they were going to settle for nothing less.

Nick Ruiz had been the youngest of Rick Pitino's coaching staff when he came in to save the Kentucky Wildcats from oblivion under the sanctions imposed by the NCAA. Tubby had been on that staff too, he'd won a title to put alongside Rick's. After that they never got past the Elite 8. Nick had won a title and was on his way to his fourth Final Four in eleven years. He was young, he was hungry, and he liked to win. And in some ways he was a lot like Rick.

Thing was, Nick wasn't commenting. Or when he did answer he hedged, sending the Big Blue Nation into a frenzy. He hadn't said yes, but he hadn't closed the door either. It didn't take a genius to figure out, that if he broke this story, he wouldn't be living on cold cereal and hot dogs one week and spaghetti at his Mom and Dad's the next. He was forty years old, and his writing career had yet to take off. But, gratefully, his parents had never told him he was wrong. Had never told him to give up. The only thing his mother had ever asked him was when was he going to get married. Now that, he could handle.

Shuffling around his house in his house robe and white

boxers he was the product of a British father and Italian mother immigrant family and he wasn't just sexy, he was beautiful. Because, even with the dreadful diet, he practiced yoga, martial arts, and ran three miles every day. He also went out to the sports bars every night, hoping to overhear some conversation, chat up some guy, or bed a lady after a long talk. The morning after was always so awkward. He'd broken quite a few hearts that way.

Sipping on his coffee he opened the paper on his table and began to read. Nothing. His blood began to pump. No story. No break. That meant he still had a chance. A chance to break out of his mundane job and his mundane existence as a manager at the local Applebees. He hated it there. He had to be a dick and he hate to be a dick. To top it off, he didn't really know his employees, and they all hated him for it. The only real bonus was that in the bar they had a huge television and they could run the games on it. He was a terrible manager, but it was a food service job and those were the ones that worked around his passion. So cold cereal, hot dogs, spaghetti, and sports bars were his life and Adam Paul Matthews, as miserable as he was two days shy of his forty-first birthday, he would not give up his dream just yet. A hot story was heading his way, he could taste it in the air.

***

Kiara Jackson hunched over the deep, stainless steel sink

filled with oversized dishes washing them with scalding, hot water. She hated her job. She hated her life. The only respite she got were her nights out at the sports bars where she could handicap every aspect of UK basketball.

"Hey Jackson, get a move on it. You're not at home. You're working."

And working for Adam Matthews was just the kicker. Almost everyone who worked at the Applebees by WalMart hated him. So in that sense she wasn't so alone. But then, she was invisible to the people there. The cooks associated with the cooks, the servers with the servers, she didn't associate with the other dishwashers and clean-up crew. Not because they were dumb or uninteresting, but because they had very little in common. Besides, she had secrets, secrets she'd rather die with rather than live and share with the Applebees community at large. At least she worked very few hours. Twelve or less. Not that she received preferential treatment, it just had a little something to do with one of those secrets. At least Adam had the decency not to go around spreading that one around.

The Final Four started tonight. Adam had promised her she would be off by five. Giving her a chance to change clothes and be at Damon's Sports Bar & Grill by five forty-five. Papers spread, meal served and coffee in hand by tip-off. As if she needed any coffee. She got wound up quite well enough on her own. She looked at the clock as the world whirled on around her.

Five after five. Clearing the sink out, Kiara dried off her hands and walked out into the bar area where one could always find Adam and tapped him on the shoulder.

"Excuse me, you said I could go at five and it's almost ten after."

"We got a rush, I need you to stay."

"First of all, that will affect my disability. Second of all, you said I could go."

"You can go when I say you can go. Now get back in the kitchen."

"Asshole," she mumbled under her breath.

"What did you just say."

"You heard me."

"No, I think I want to hear it again."

"If you insist, I called you an asshole. You promised me something then you went back on it."

"Just because you're crazy doesn't mean you get cart blanche around here."

Kiara's face turned red.

"Justine. Hit me."

"Justine, if you know what's good for you, you'll ignore her order."

Justine was probably, who up to this point, had been the only one who knew Kiara's secret. She was a tall, beautiful red head who everyone liked. Especially the guys. But she had nothing to do with them. She was a lesbian and preferred Kate Winslet to George Clooney.

"Here you go Ki," she said handing Kiara a mug full of the house red wine, "use it wisely."

"If you go any further with this consider both of yourselves fired."

Kiara hesitated. She didn't mind being without a job. But Justine had always been nice to her.

"Don't worry about me Ki, I'll be just fine. Do what you need to."

Still she hesitated. She wasn't one for reckless acts of anger unless she was tired, manic, or if someone had really set her off, and it seemed as if Adam had gone for the triple play Instead of throwing it in his face she dumped it on his shoes. His eyes closed and his jaw clenched.

"Fuck the firing shit, I quit. Here's the glass Justine. I hope everything thing works out for you and everyone else here. Even you Adam Paul."

She turned and walked out the front door. She could only guess that he was fuming. The piece of crap men in her life were always fuming when she finally left. Even her first psychiatrist had been pissed when she left him for another professional. Oh well. She was without a job and alone again. Just another shitty day in paradise.

***

Kiara watched as everyone around her drank, ate, and watched the big game between the Gators and the Bruins for a chance to go to the final. The Big Dance. A part of her hoped the Gators would lose. Perhaps leaving the chance open that Nick Ruiz would come to the 'Cats as opposed to staying in Florida. One could hope, right?

"I guess I owe you an apology don't I."

She twisted her head up at the sound of Adam's voice. It made the anger and embarrassment from just an hour before burn fresh in her heart and mind. He had exposed her in a way she felt was unforgivable, and now he was here, asking for her forgiveness.

"Are you going to yell at me?"

"Why should I? I said all I had to say at the restaurant."

"True, but I was wrong to handle the situation the way I did. There are better ways to go about getting what you want out of people, I'm just not good at it."

"It's not that you're not good at it Adam, it's that you don't care."

He flinched.

"Fair enough. Why don't you let me buy you a drink."

"I got coffee. The refills are free. But if you really want to sit and talk to me, sit. Just don't mess my system up."

Adam smiled.

"What system?"

"My handicapping system. The Bruins and the Gators are pretty well matched. So I give the game a five point spread in Florida's favor."

"Can I have a look at this?"

"Sure, just don't. Mess it. Up."

Sliding into the booth he found himself close to the rough and tumble Kiara Jackson. He had never been this close to her before. She actually had a lovely face. Porcelain skin. Soft brown eyes. And a small nose, with perfect lips. Too bad she had a little extra cushioning on her. He wasn't a chubby chaser. Never had been, and he wasn't about to start now.

"You're judging me."

"What are you talking about? I'm looking at your handicapping abilities."

"You gave me a look. And I don't know what it was for. But I know when I'm being judged and you were judging me. Lord knows I have a litany of things to be judged for, but after tonight at work, I don't feel up to it."

She was right. And if she knew what he had judged her on it would hurt her. That kind of stuff cut a woman deep. Of course, he'd cut her pretty deep not that long ago.

"I'm sorry if I did anything. Sometimes I just get a look on my face."

"Now you're lying. And you're not very good at it either. Why don't you get a drink, look at my work, and watch the game. We can jut avoid the emotional landmines for now."

"So you're forgiving me?"

"Now you're just hearing things."

Adam chuckled.

"You know, you could give me an apology."

"Now you're just dreaming."

"Maybe," he said with a smile, looking down at her brackets. He stopped cold. With two or three exceptions she had filled them out perfectly. "What are you, some kind of savant?"

"Nope, I just do my homework."

Perhaps the story wasn't just in Nick Ruiz. Maybe it was in Big Blue Nation itself. Maybe it was in Kiara Jackson, the biggest fan he'd come across in years.

Chapter Two

The press conference had been hell on earth. He was being
courted by the Wildcats while he was on a red hot run through the
tournament with his team of eleven years, the Florida Gators.
Nick Ruiz loved his team, loved his boys, loved his job. But even
though he'd taken them to four Final Fours, and was on the verge
of perhaps back to back national titles, he still couldn't sell
out his 12,000 seat arena. He was at a school where football
would always be king, and to be honest, it hurt his pride more
than he'd liked to admit.

At Kentucky, however, basketball was God, and nothing would

ever usurp the Big Blue Nation's worshiping of it. Heady stuff. But if you couldn't deliver, God help you. He'd watched what the Nation had done to his former mentor Tubby Smith and wished that kind of life on nobody. But the offer was oh so tempting.

"Honey, come to bed. It's late," his wife Rhiannon called.

She was beautiful. Long, chestnut, colored hair, large, silver blue eyes. That and she was from Kentucky. He'd met her while coaching under Pitino there. And she loved basketball as much as he did. She was pregnant now with their first child, a little girl. Five months to be exact. The only thing he loved more than basketball and his wife, was the baby. When he couldn't sleep at night he would snuggle with her and touch her belly, hoping he would know what to do when time came for the baby to arrive. Right now, though, it was all about the tournament and he had to force all thoughts of the baby and Kentucky from his mind. For now, at least, he was the head coach of the Florida Gators and his job was to win a national championship with them.

***

Kiara barreled down the road tears streaming down her face without a clue as how to explain this to her case worker, Mya.

Mya had placed her in three different jobs in the last nine months, and each time something happened to create a vacancy with her being the one who created it. What made it worse was that Adam had come up to her and apologized and joked with her like they were old friends. They weren't old friends. They were enemies and that was that. Maybe she would get lucky and Justine would leave a message and they could hang out. They could commiserate. Oh who the fuck was she kidding? Justine wasn't going to get fired, Adam had too much of a hard on for her. In that respect he was just like the other guys who worked at Applebees for him.

But he had been funny. And he had been nice. At Damon's. Maybe he just hated his job. She did, or had. She hated every job she had and she hated herself for it. Once upon a time she could work a job she liked during the day while pursing her passion during the night. But it had been eight years since she'd even played a note. She didn't see the status quo changing anytime soon. Crazy. Lonely. Jobless. Alone Kiara Jackson.

Stop it she told herself. Pity didn't do anyone any good. Including herself. Her cell phone began to ring. Who would be calling her this late at night?

"Hello?"

"Ki?" came a teary voice.

"That depends. Who is this?"

A few short, uncontrolled breaths followed by sniffles greeted her ears.

"Justine?"

"I don't have anyone else to call."

Great, the friend of last resort. The go-to friend.

"That's all right. I don't mind. Calm down and tell me what's wrong."

More sniffles, more tears.

"I was leaving work and Horatio asked me if I wanted to get a drink at the Hotel. When I said no he tried to rape me."

A cold knot formed in Kiara's stomach. Secrets. Was Justine giving her the entire story?

"Did you call the police?"

"I'm at the station now."

"Do you need a ride somewhere?"

"I was wondering if I could crash at your place for the

night."

Kiara's family was always accusing her of not being close to anyone, yet willing to give the shirt off her back to the first person who needed it. Justine needed it. At least, she said she did. And from what she knew of her Justine wasn't one to lie about such things.

"What about your girlfriend, Lynn? Why not call her?"

"We broke up last week. Please Ki."

Kiara didn't want to, but if it was at all possible Justine had had the worse night.

"Sure, you can crash at my place."

"Oh Ki?"

"Yeah?"

"I need a ride too."

"That's not a problem."

"You're a good person."

"You don't need to say that to get my help."

"Maybe not, but you've had a rotten day too."

"Just sit tight. We can talk about it when I pick you up."

"Ki?"

"Yeah Justine?"

"Thanks."

Kiara sat in silence. She didn't mind being the go to friend, she just wished she had one.

* * *

Nick had awakened to the sense of nervous anticipation of what was to hopefully be the second of back to back championships. It was only six thirty in the morning, but it was time for him and his staff to start going over tapes of UCLA and how they had been getting passed everything the tournament and regular season had thrown at him. Rhiannon reached for him as he rolled out of bed.

"Don't go."

He kissed her hand, then kissed her cheek.

"Duty calls honey. I have to go."

"Five more minutes."

"I'm on my boys and coaches to always be on time. I can't be late. Especially not now."

She turned her back to him.

"Then go."

"Come on Rhiannon, don't do this now."

"I'm pregnant. The least you can do is give me five minutes."

"I'll have five minutes when the tournament is done."

"Don't lie to me. Then you'll be considering that carrot on a stick every reporter has been salivating about."

"I'm leaving now. You knew that this was what I wanted to do with my life when you married me. I thought you understood that."

"You're as obsessed with this game as my father ever dared to be."

"And you say that like it's a bad thing. Go back to sleep. You'll feel better at the game tonight. After we win."

"You go win. I'll play the wife. And in the end we'll all be happy."

Her voice had drifted and he heard the light snore on her breath. He loved his wife. But sometimes he wondered how they'd ever stayed together as long as they had.

***

Adam was nervous as he stood at Kiara's door with a bouquet of white carnations. She'd been upset when she left the bar the night before. Even though she'd opened up like a book when it came to basketball she'd steered clear of the incident at Applebees. He'd sensed a very sad and lonely woman. He wondered if anyone really knew her, or had taken the time to get to know her. Firing her was the right thing to do, but how he'd done was unacceptable. Calling her crazy, exposing her vulnerability in the worst kind of way. He was a heel for doing it and he owed it to her to make amends. Far past buying her a drink and talking basketball with her. Now he stood at her apartment door, flowers in hand, and wondering how anyone could live in a bigger dump than he did. He knocked.

The door swung open and a disheveled Kiara answered. She looked shocked.

"What are you doing here?"

He held out the flowers.

"I'm here to apologize."

"I thought you did that last night."

"I was a real ass. I think you deserve more than a drink."

"What? You going to be my friend now?"

She was being a bitch, but he bit his tongue and tried to

remember that he'd fired the first shot in this particular fight.

"At the risk of sounding like a ten year old, I'd like to try. I'm not sorry I fired you, but I am sorry for calling you crazy. You're not crazy and you didn't deserve to be exposed like that. And if you would take these as a peace offering I would appreciate it."

"I shouldn't forgive you, you know."

He bit his tongue again, she was right. She shouldn't.

"But there is a way to make it up to me."

He couldn't help but smile.

"What's that?"

"Fire Horatio."

"Why would I do that? He's my best cook and server."

"You fire him because he assaulted Justine in the parking lot last night after they closed the restaurant."

"Take these," he said, thrusting the flowers into her hands. He dug his cell phone out of his pocket, "can I come in?"

"Sure, why not. But be quiet. Justine just finally went to sleep and Lynn is on her way over."

Stepping in he was confused.

"I thought they broke up."

"Boy was I out of the loop."

"Girls talk and boys fantasize."

"And what am I?"

"A woman who doesn't gossip."

Kiara blushed.

"Trust me, Adam, if I had anyone to gossip to I would."

"No Kiara, I don't think that you would. Has she filed a police report?"

"Yeah. I guess I don't have to ask you what you did with your evening once I left last night."

She walked into her kitchenette and pulled down a vase and placed the carnations in water. Reaching high above her head she got down two bowls.

"I should be offended."

"I'm not judging you. I'm just making small talk. What do you want? Oatmeal or a breakfast bowl?"

"Either is better than what I eat."

"What do you eat?"

"Captain Crunch."

"Man your pay must be as shitty as mine was. Now sit."

"Oatmeal."

"Flavored or plain?"

"What are you? My wife?"

For a moment she seemed stung by his words and he wished he could eat them, shove them back into his mouth.

"I'm trying to be your friend. But if you'd rather I didn't, you can take a seat and watch me eat my oatmeal in peace. Or you could just leave altogether."

He stepped forward and placed a calming hand on her shoulder.

"Look, I don't know what's happened to you in your life to make you so scared of people, but you should know, I'm not going to hurt you."

"Oh really."

"Really. Give me a second chance. I can be a good friend if you just give me try."

She wanted to give him a chance. God she wanted to give him a chance. But he had been such an asshole.

"Well..."

A fast knock at the door startled them both.

"That must be Lynn."

She walked over to the door and opened it without looking through the peephole. Horatio pushed his way in, sending Kiara reeling back on her heels.

"I need to see her."

"Get out. After what you did you're not going to be seeing anybody."

"You stupid bitch. You think you can keep her from me? Justine and me have something special."

Adam stepped from the shadows and grabbed Horatio by the neck. And threw him out the door.

"The next time I even see you I'm calling the cops."

"What lies did that crazy tell you about me?

"You're fired Horatio. I've seen the police report and the EPO. Your check will be mailed to you. And if I even suspect you're sniffing around Kiara or Justine, I'll pay a special visit to your parents."

Horatio pointed at Kiara and smiled.

"Your knight can't be here all the time."

Anger shook her body as she fly-kicked Horatio right under the chin and sent him stumbling into the guard rail.

"Sleep with one eye open mother fucker, I've faced much bigger demons than you and I think I can handle myself. Now get the hell out of here before I call the cops."

Blood poured from his nose and lip.

"Crazy bitch."

Kiara slammed the door shut and ran to the garbage pail. Holding her hair back she began to retch. Adam came up behind her and took her hair in one hand and rubbed her back with the other. He could say something, but nothing that wouldn't sound trite in the face of what had just happened.

When the retching stopped she began to cry. Adam lifted her to a standing position and took her in his arms. As she shook violently in them he could only think about who or what had left such a mark on her. And it made him mad. So mad he wanted to find them and put a mark of his own on them.

***

"Listen, I've got to go to work. What do you say I drop by later and we watch the game? Have a little takeout, get your mind off of things."

"I'm unemployed, how would I do that?" Kiara asked.

"Then how about I pick you up and we do it at my place?"

For the first time since they'd met Adam watched her smile with a sweetness he hadn't thought possible.

"Seriously?"

"Yeah," he paused, "seriously."

"What if Horatio brings his nasty ass around here again?"

"You call me. And I'll come."

"No matter what?"

"That's what friends do, right?"

Another smile.

"It's been a long time since I've had any friends. You're not just yanking me around are you?"

He smiled back.

"After the beat down I just watched you give Horatio? I wouldn't dare."

Chapter Three

The weather was chilly and misting. An unlikely day to visit
the Oakdale cemetery in Louisville, Kentucky. But Kiara didn't
care. She visited often and picked days when she thought no one
else would be there. Some people found peace in a sanctuary. She
found it in Oakdale. She found it there because her best friend

Crista Fellows was buried there.

Just close your eyes Kiara, and everything you've ever wanted will be within your grasp.

Crista was always such a dreamer, she just never had anyone from her family who believed in her dreams. She made Kiara believe in her dreams and Crista's family hated Kiara for it. That was okay, she hated them. She knew the score. And when they'd shunned her at Crista's funeral it had not surprised her. But the pain had been excruciating nonetheless. Standing at Crista's grave she didn't cry. She was at peace. She was standing with her sister. The old saying was blood was thicker than water, but not in the case with Crista, they were each others lifelines. Even now, when Crista was gone from the earth, they shared a bond, there was a comfort in that. It let her know, that here, in Oakdale, Crista was close by, and that anytime Kiara needed her she could come and visit and touch the friendship they had once shared.

"God I wish you were here Crista."

She closed her eyes and remembered the last time she was with Crista when she was really alive. Last year, in the middle of the 1997-98 basketball season, she had bought tickets to the Duke-UK game. They had driven to Chapel Hill to see the match-up. They'd gotten a room at the most luxurious hotel, and they's made signs and like crazies they'd painted their faces blue and white. *We gotta do this more often*, Crista had said, both of them knowing this was probably the first and last time they'd ever do something like that together. The Wildcats lost in a heartbreaker, 82-81. It wouldn't have been so bad----oh who was she kidding? Losing to Duke always sucked. Bunch of rich, spoiled, self-entitled, little boys who had no clue as to what the real world was like. Crista's little sister was like that, come to think of it, her whole family thought that she, Kiara, was like that.

It angered her. To have to grieve alone. To have people think she didn't matter. Her family, the Jackson family, would have her living in a trailer with a husband and six kids right now. The worse the husband the better. Someone had to keep her in line. Somehow she'd broken free of all that and found Crista. Crista had been her family for ten years. A deep ache formed in her chest and she thought she might cry. She hadn't had to grieve alone this morning, a surprise angel had arrived at her doorstep extending a hand in friendship. And man, she had taken it. Without a hint of hesitation she had held on for dear life. Adam Paul Matthews? Boss. Friend? Friend. Maybe.

*　*　*

Adam's head pounded. The rage was welling up in him like an untapped source waiting to break free. It occurred to him he didn't know Kiara at all. She was more than the chubby girl with a pretty face who did the dishes. Who, because of him, was now unemployed.

He couldn't hire her back, his handling of that moment and her reaction to it had sealed her fate on that one. What was he thinking reaching out to her like that? Women always wanted more than friendship, but it was clear that if anyone ever needed friendship it was Kiara. The only one who ever gave her the time of day at work was Justine. And even that was peripheral at best.

Where most of his employees would pair off on their breaks, or sit at the bar and talk to Justine, Kiara sat in the same corner booth, eating a sack lunch and pouring over basketball statistics. And the team she loved the most, even when they were

struggling, was UK. So it was on pins and needles she watched
tonight's game, hoping against all hope, that Nick Ruiz was
making it his swan song with the Florida Gators.

The anger was beginning to ebb as he forced himself to think
about what he knew about Kiara beyond the game of basketball. She
was the least pretentious of the lot he had working for him, and
ironically, the one who had given him the least amount of trouble
up until last night. She kept her hair black and half way down
her back. She never did anything special with it, just looped
back in a ponytail, tied away from her face. And the eyes, which
had been filled with anger with him, had turned into a caged
beast's as she fly-kicked the now unemployed Horatio Thomas to
her balcony railing. But she had pain. Deep pain. And even though
he hadn't expected it to, it had touched him. She had cried so
hard and so long, it hurt him. The kind of pain she was choking
on should be reserved for asses like himself or monsters like
Horatio. She was strong, but she was alone. And no one deserved
to be alone. His cell phone rang.

"Hello."

"Um, Adam?"

He stopped at the light.

"Speaking."

"It's Justine."

"Is everything all right? Horatio bothering you?"

"No, not me. The hospital just called me."

"About what? If you're fine, why are you calling me?"

"It's Kiara."

"What hospital?"

"Baptist East, but Adam, I have to warn you, it's pretty bad."

The light changed, he pressed down on the gas.

"I'll kill him."

"It wasn't Horatio."

He swerved in an out traffic and took the ramp to I-65 South.

"Then who the hell was it?"

Dead silence greeted his ears.

"Tell me Justine who was it?"

"She was mumbling the name Junior."

"Who's Junior? Does he work for me?"

"You brought her flowers and you don't know who Junior is?"

"Damn it Justine!"

"Okay, okay. He's one of her uncles, and she is terrified of him."

Adam took a few deep breaths as he sped down the highway.

"Where'd they find her?"

"By her car outside the Oakdale cemetery."

"Why would she be there?"

"That you'll have to ask her, but like I said, it's bad Adam. I'm here and I've already made it known that she has an EPO out on her family, so you'll have to show i.d. I put your name down on the list of acceptable visitors."

"Justine, how did you find out about this?"

"Before she went into a coma she said two names mine and yours."

"How do they know we're not under the EPO?"

"After I told them, the police ran it through their records."

"Tell me something, what does this 'Junior' look like?"

"There'll time enough for that later. Right now, if you have any shred of decency you'll just come up here and be there for her."

"What about you?"

"I'm staying until you get here, then I have a shift I have to work or my rent doesn't get paid. But I want Kiara to know she does have friends in the plural."

"I wish I hadn't been such an ass."

"Don't worry about it. We all have our moments. Just get here okay? I get the distinct feeling it's your face she'll want to see when she wakes up."

"Why's that?"

"Because you came to her and asked to be her friend. Where I just called her and asked her to clean up my mess when I could've just called Lynn and she would have come just as easily."

"You flatter me Justine. I'll make it up to you. What room is she in?"

"Go to registration, tell them who you are and who you're there to see. They'll send you back and I'll leave."

He didn't want to think about what Junior had done to Kiara. His face grew hot at the thought of how much pain she was in. *I'm coming Kiara. You have friends. Just hold on. I'm coming.*

***

Nick had pushed the argument with Rhiannon from his mind. He had to. For now he had to focus on the game at hand. His boys, the national spotlight, the pressure, hell, the pure adrenaline of the night was too much to resist. So for now, the wife would have to wait.

"Nick, the boys are waiting," his assistant George Hanson said tapping him on the shoulder.

Nick hadn't realized he'd been so lost in thought. He had to get a handle on himself if he expected to do his job tonight. He wanted his kids to live in this moment, to relish it, to savor it. It wasn't often in sports for a team to get a chance to repeat. Especially in collegiate basketball with kids going pro early, and the me and I factor working against the coach. The showboat factor was high. Nick Ruiz didn't stand for any showboating. It was snotty, it was arrogant, and it sullied the game. He hated it. And when he saw it, it was grounds for benching. But kids liked to showboat, and well, this was the tournament, a little showboating never hurt anyone, right?

"Nick," George said a bit louder this time.

"Coming, are they waiting?"

George was a short, round, man with shocking white hair. He'd been with Nick since his UMass days when he was just a player running the floor. Not the most talented player, but he could read a court with the best of them. George loved Nick like a son, even if he didn't agree with the way he was handling all the UK press. Nick should just come out and say he wasn't going to UK and that he was thrilled with Florida.

So what if he had only sold out a 12,000 seat arena eight times in eleven years. So what if Florida was always going to be a football state. And so what if, no matter how many championships he won national or conference he would never be as big on campus as he would be at UK if he won like he won at Florida.

That was the thing though, how badly did he want to stay at Florida? Hopefully as much as he did. He loved the boys. He loved the way even though there was pressure, it wasn't microscopic pressure. But now was not the time for that discussion. Now was the time for national glory and victory. And if anyone had earned it, it was this team.

    Boxer. Newton. Hunchford. Kelly. Names that should live in the annals of college basketball history. But might not because their names were not Duke. North Carolina. Or even UCLA. George hoped Nick stayed. The bitterness he would imbue at the school would be heavy, and every time he stepped into that gym, into his house, he would be booed. Like Pitino in Lexington, there would be bitterness. Ones that felt he was a traitor for stepping over to the other side.

    As he and Nick walked into the locker room and found their team waiting, George watched Nick work his magic on the boys and lift their spirits up and cajole them into battle. Because that was what the NCAA national title game was. The final battle in a sixty-four team war, where the winner was treated like a God. And if you were from a basketball state you were the biggest God of all, especially if you were coaching UK.

    "All right. This is your moment. Live in it. Taste it. Seize it. Because something like it might never come your way ever again. Boys, today you are men, and don't ever let anyone tell you different. On three."

Every warrior gathered round, hand pressed to hand and shouted in an ear ringing chorus.

"One! Two! Three! Team!"

Their hands dropped to the center and they ran out pumped and ready to defend their national championship title. Nick followed them out focused and ready to coach, the UK job offer just a nagging blip in the back of his mind. But it was there, a light pulse with the potential to become a major distraction.

Chapter Four

It was late. Adam had no idea how long he'd been sitting there at Kiara's bedside. Just that he'd become attached to the employee in a very short amount of time. And Justine had been right, it was bad.

A broken arm, broken fingernails, a cracked rib, a busted up lip, a concussion, bruises and contusions and two sprained ankles. They had taken her off the respirator and expected her to die. But she hadn't.

So he had put on a surgical gown and taken her bruised hand in his and prayed to a God who had seemed to have abandoned Kiara, to spare her life.

"I know I've been a dick, God. And that I've been a dick to Kiara. But she's been through too much to take her now. She's a good person. I promise to protect her. Just spare her and I'll live my life right. I swear."

Nothing. He looked at the time. Nine-thirty. *The game*. He started to stand-up and kissed her forehead. He walked out into the corridor and up to the nurse's desk. He smiled.

"My friend is in room 435. I was wondering could we get a television. We had plans to watch the Florida/UCLA game tonight. And I know she isn't awake, but it was important that we watch this game together."

The nurse was young and pretty, and very tired. She looked down at her sheet.

"You're with Kiara Jackson, right?"

"Right."

"Lucky girl."

He smiled, "No, lucky me."

That seemed to do the trick.

"Let me see what I can do. Just go back to the room. It wouldn't do to have her waking up without her friend would it?"

He smiled, "No, I guess it wouldn't. Listen..."

"Don't worry, from what I can tell she needs every angel she can get on her side."

"Thanks."

He turned and returned to Kiara's room and sat back down beside her, taking her hand again.

"Hey, I'm such a good friend I'm going to keep our plans tonight. Florida/UCLA. Nick Ruiz, the hot Latino coach who might be coming to UK? The nurse is bringing us a television to watch it on."

The door opened and the nurse wheeled in the t.v. She looked at the way Mr. Matthews was looking down at Kiara Jackson. Such concern. Such kindness. Such compassion. Lucky girl. She didn't care what Mr. Matthews said.

"Here you go. Channel five right?"

He continued to look down at Kiara.

"Yeah, right."

"There you go."

"Thank you. I really needed to keep my promise to her."

"I understand. If you need anything just press the button."

"Okay," he said stroking her hand lightly with his thumb.

Lucky girl, she thought.

Lucky him, he thought, how had he lucked out to find such a friend.

                                    ***

Nick could feel the nerves in his kids at halftime. They

were leading by eleven points, and they just wanted to win so bad. So did he. If he did, he could say, without a doubt, that he had done everything he could possibly do for the University of Florida and legitimately look at the offer from Kentucky without feeling like he was betraying his boys. As he looked at them one by one he realized the only way they would not feel betrayed by him was if he stayed. Four of his starters were seniors. They were on their way to being grown men, they would perhaps understand better than the rest that there were times when larger goals lay out on the horizon before you. UK was the crown jewel of college basketball royalty and he wanted to go. But right now, in the present, he was the head coach of the Florida Gators and they needed him to be there for them.

"Boxer, you need to look for the pass more. You're doing a good job, but champions are great. So look for the pass, all right? And Newton, block out, watch going over the back. The refs haven't been calling it, but you know how this sport goes, and you know how John Clougherty is. Hunchford, stop the showboating. I don't care if you invent the mother of all dunks. You know how I feel about it."

"But Coach-"

"Excuse me?" Nick's voice suddenly rose to a booming, ear shattering level.

"Nothing."

"No Hunchford. I think we all want to hear what you have to say."

Hunchford was somewhere between contrite and sullen.

"Answer me!"

"I didn't mean anything by it Coach. It's just that it's the title game, and we've worked so hard and..."

"And what? You deserve a little play time? How many of you here agree with him? That you can showboat now that you have a national audience? Go ahead raise your fucking hands if you think that it's time to play. Because the last time I checked there were still twenty God damn minutes left on the clock before we can say anything about who we are and where we stand. So if you think it's time to showboat then feel free to leave this locker room. And let me make one thing perfectly clear, if you do leave you will not receive a ring, you will not be allowed back on the team. You will be an afterthought on ESPN. Do I make myself clear?"

"Yes Coach!" they all shouted in unison.

"Listen to me, you're only twenty minutes away from making history. It's been fifteen years since Duke did it. And you've got a hundred times more talent and class than they ever dreamed of having. So what are we?!"

"Team!"

"Who are we?!"

"The Gators?!"

"And what is our destiny?!"

"Champions!"

"Get out there and take care of business!"

His boys leapt up from their seats and barreled down the corridor to greatness. The next twenty minutes would determine all of their destinies. Whether he was with Florida or at Kentucky he would always be remembered as the man who built a dynasty from the ground up. And that was most satisfying.

***

The game was almost over and Kiara had yet to open her eyes, utter a word, or squeeze his hand. It was getting to be midnight and he wondered how he was going to juggle his work schedule if she needed someone to sit with her indefinitely.

"I know you're in there Kiara, wake up. Your coach is on his way to Kentucky. Just open your eyes and see it. We're friends, right? Right?"

She coughed, hard and gasped for breath. She opened her eyes and started to cry. His eyes watered.

"That's right, look at me."

"Where's Crista?"

"I don't know."

She cried some more, this time even harder. He placed his hand at her forehead.

"What's wrong?"

"He took her from me. He took my best friend and my only family from me."

"Who took Crista from you?"

Her tears turned angry.

"God did, he wouldn't let me go to her. She was standing there, waiting for me and he wouldn't let me in."

Her pain was so deep, her grief so raw her wanted to touch

her soul and heal her. But he didn't know how.

"I know I'm chopped liver at the moment, but I'm really glad you're back. Watching the game without you was no fun at all."

She was confused and disoriented, but she saw Adam with tears in his eyes, and he was holding her hand. Had he been the tug to come back she'd felt even with Crista standing there waiting for her? Impossible. Then an icy pick of fear pierced her heart.

"Where is he?"

"Who?"

All the color in her face drained itself from her cheeks. She refused to speak.

"Junior isn't going to hurt you. He can't. Not on my watch."

He watched as the tears spilled down her cheeks. He wiped them away with his thumb.

"I'm your friend, I know the circumstances are strange, but I'm here for you."

"You don't understand, I fought him. And he still got me. I fought him as hard as I've fought anybody. I hurt him. And he still got his hands on me."

A knot formed in his stomach.

"What did he do to hurt you?"

A quiet moment followed by even softer words.

"Everything, Adam. Everything."

The knot in his stomach moved into his throat.

"What's everything, Kiara?"

"My whole life," she cried.

"What's your whole life? Before the doctors come, what's your whole life?"

She covered her face with her hand and began to cry harder. What could she tell him that he couldn't figure out on his own?

"I can't say it. I've never been able to say it. Not even to Crista, she just knew. Please don't make me say it. Not now. I can't."

She began to convulse with tears. Adam felt his heart break for her. She had no one. Just him and Justine. And he had been the one to stay with her. She continued to sob. It ripped his heart out.

He eased onto her bed and gathered her up into his arms and held her gently in his arms. One day she would be ready to talk, and he was going to make sure he was the one there when she was.

* * *

Victory was sweet. Bittersweet. But sweet nonetheless. Nick Ruiz was on top of the world. And he liked it there. He just hoped at Kentucky they didn't tear him down before he could get there again. Boxer. Newton. Hunchford. Kelly. Those were his boys. They might as well be his blood. But it was time for him to move on. For them as well. Them to the pros. Him to his destiny.

"Hey Coach, it's your turn to climb the ladder," Newton shouted.

"Yeah! Cut down the nets Coach!" Boxer yelled.

"Cut 'em down!" the rest of them chimed in.

Sweet. So sweet. He climbed the steps into the air and snipped the nylon off. Completing the circle. He waved it in the air and smiled. He gazed down at his wife. She was smiling. Their argument from this morning forgotten. This was what it was for. All the sacrifice. All the hard work. All the mornings when he couldn't stay and have coffee, or when he missed dinner. He smiled back at her. Florida Gators NCAA Men's Division I Basketball Champions. Nick Ruiz head coach, for the Kentucky

Wildcats, for the Big Blue Nation.

***

"Why are you here?"

"Because I'm you're friend," Adam said holding her hand.

She liked how it felt. His large, strong, hand, holding her soft, bruised, and battered one. Like a prince come to save the damsel in distress. She hated those stories. She wanted to be anything but one of those stories. Yet here she was with a man, who had, by his own admission was glad to have her back. Of course, he was calling her friend, but his touch was kind and his words were, well, they were like night from day from the guy who had been her boss.

"No. Why are you really here? We've known each other for how long? And this whole friends thing didn't start until this morning."

Adam paused, without thinking he licked his lips. He noticed how much trouble Kiara was having keeping her eyes on him. He touched her face, she pulled away.

"That's not fair and it isn't funny."

"I wasn't trying to be."

"Adam, you've proven you're a really nice guy. But when you do things like that it makes me like you."

"Is that such a bad thing?"

"It wouldn't be if I hadn't overheard you talking to Horatio once about how you thought fat girls were gross and ugly. And that he only reason you'd ever fuck one is if you were drunk or felt sorry for them. And I saw the way you looked at me the other night when you came to the bar."

"And how did I look at you?"

"Like it was to bad I had such a pretty face on such a fat body."

Was he that transparent? Had that really crossed his face? He liked her. Genuinely. In her bravery he was even attracted to her. His heart ached for her. It wasn't pity that he felt for her. It was compassion.

"I'm sorry for that, I had no right to talk as if you were not there. And I had no right to look at you as if you were too stupid to pick up on what I was thinking. But you've got to believe me when I say that I like you. And that I don't pity you. You inspire me, Kiara. That makes me want to be your friend even more."

She wanted to believe him. She wanted to accept his apology. But how many apologies had she heard in her lifetime?

"When I say that I like you do you even understand what I'm saying?"

Of course he did. This was the first night in ages he had not used to get something out of the opposite sex. Tears glistened in her eyes.

"Of course you do. You're just sparing my feelings."

Placing his hand on her cheek he sweetly kissed her damaged lips and pulled away. In a roughened, low voice he gave her a spark of hope, a moment of joy.

"If I didn't like you, I would say so. Especially right now."

She reached up and touched his cheek, running her thumb over his lips, before she drew it back, he caught it with a gently and pressed her tender flesh to his mouth.

"Whore," a female voice hissed.

Kiara stiffened, Adam whipped his head around.

"You have no right to be here, leave."

Kiara's commanding voice caught him off guard. What had been a soft, intimate moment was being shattered by an intruder who was probably not on the list.

"You seduce my brother, then cry rape? I should bend you over my knee right here."

"Leave."

"You have no right to tell me to do anything. I'm your mother."

"You're dead to me."

"The hell I am," she started to step inside the room.

Adam rose to his feet.

"You heard the lady. Now leave before I suggest to her that she notify the police that you're violating a court order."

"And just who do you think you are?"

"I'm the one you're going to have to answer to if you don't get out of here."

The woman froze, and seemed to be debating her odds of getting passed him.

"You can't avoid us forever, Ki. And him. Like he actually cares about doing anything for you other than getting in your pants."

Adam walked forward, shoved Kiara's mother out the door and shut it.

"You didn't have to do that."

He smiled and joined her back on the bed.

"Somebody had to, and you just needed a little help from someone who cares."

"You care?"

"I care."

Pushing Kiara's hair back he nuzzled her neck and breathed her in.

"I care very much."

Burying her hand in his hair she sighed. She didn't know what this meant, or where it was going. But she was tired of being alone. And for now she wasn't alone.

Chapter Five

The healing process along with the physical therapy was murder, but it wasn't like Kiara couldn't do it. Her ankles were what hurt her the worst, which was surprising considering what all her injuries were. She had grit and she fought for each step. And at the end of each day, there stood her friend, Adam Paul Matthews. She was a lucky girl. Especially when he told her he was the lucky one.

"I'm sick of this shit. I'm ready to go home."

"I'm sure you are. But you have to be able to defend yourself."

There he was with that annoying sense of reason again. She smiled though gritted teeth as she held on to the bars and walked forward one painful step at a time.

"I thought you were going to protect me?"

"Of course I am. But you're no helpless Hannah are you?"

"Fuck you," she said laughing through the pain.

"Ah, promises, promises."

"You are not-you are not-you are not funny."

He laughed with a full booming laugh.

Sweat lined her brow as she completed the walk and collapsed into the physical therapist's arms.

"Okay Miss Jackson. That's enough for today, let's sit down here," Betty set her down into the wheelchair and smiled at Adam. "I do believe she's the hardest working patient I've had in a long time."

"Does that mean I get to go home soon?"

Betty looked at Kiara and gave her a conspiratorial grin.

"You know that's not up to me."

"Yes, but I also know your recommendation could go a long way to getting me out of here."

"You'll be out of here soon enough. We want you strong enough to take care of yourself since you don't have any next of kin listed on your chart."

"I'll never get out of here if that's the case," Kiara laughed, "oh well, that's better than having a next of kin who would just land me in here again."

Adam admired her sense of humor, and understood her itch to get out of the hospital.

"What if I was put down as her emergency contact?"

Betty's eyes sparkled.

"There's a good chance she could go home with you."

"Ah hell no," Kiara said with a smile.

"And why not?" Adam said with mock indignation.

"Because you're a guy and I'm a girl and well, I hardly know you."

"I promise to treat you with greatest amount of respect a guy has ever treated you with."

"Then you're definitely not going to be my emergency contact."

His voice softened, as did his eyes.

"I can arrange things so that not only that you're safe, but that you can keep you're privacy and independence as well."

Betty was astounded.

"I say take it Miss Jackson."

A smile played on Kiara's lips. How funny, in the last week Adam had become her constant companion. Sleeping at the hospital, coming to her after he got off from work, making sure no one from her family would touch her or hurt her. She was a lucky girl. She'd even scored a sweet kiss and a few intimate moments with him. However, she knew better than to read anything into them. Adam wasn't the type to fall in love that quickly. Besides, she wasn't his type anyway. She was much too chunky for his liking. So she would just enjoy his friendship.

"What would I have to do?"

"Well," she said, "because of your ankles you would need constant care."

"What about my rib?"

"You've already proven, even with a fractured femur and a cracked rib, that you have the spirit to push ahead with a tough PT schedule. If he signs on as your emergency contact he's saying that he is partially responsible for getting you here and making sure you do your at home PT."

"She can just stay with me."

"Oh hon, I don't know how close you two are, but I would jump on that offer."

Kiara laughed a full throated laugh as she threw her head back before coming back up with a smile.

"With all the shit I've been through, I think I'm going to say yes. On one condition."

"What's that?" he asked.

"You know my cat you've been checking up on?"

"Yeah."

"We pick her up and she stays with us until I'm able to take care of myself."

He grinned, "Wouldn't have it any other way."

"So," Kiara asked turning to Betty, "what are you going to tell the doctor?"

"I can't promise anything, but I'll put in a good word and I'll tell him that you have a friend who's willing to help out with your physical therapy."

Kiara blushed under Adam's gaze and smile. She was lucky. For the second time in her life God had blessed her with a friend who was willing to be a lifeline. He must've been able to read her thoughts because when he walked over to her he bent over and whispered in her ear.

"No, Kiara. I'm lucky. And don't you forget it."

***

The frenzy around his decision was intense. The spotlight greater than he'd anticipated. He and his wife had talked over where he wanted to spend the rest of his college career at length and Kentucky had been the subject at hand. Nick Ruiz knew in his hear that was where he wanted to go. Where he could bring the Wildcats back to the prominence the fans demanded they be at. But he looked at the mess his friend had left and wondered just how badly he wanted the job. Rhiannon also pointed out what the fans had done to the coaches who had won championships only to be snubbed by the fanbase.

But Ruiz knew the desire that burned in the Big Blue Nation's heart, it burned in his. The challenge was great, the chance for glory and passion and adoration, even greater, but he had to look at the dark side.

Websites had popped up. Petitions had been passed around. All with the intention of pushing Tubby Smith out of his coaching position. If he did not win, Big Blue Nation would turn on him like a pit of rattlesnakes and barbarians calling for nothing less than his head on a spike. The question was, could he deliver what they wanted?

And what they wanted was a top twenty season and a legitimate shot at the Final Four every year. If he were honest with himself some of the more boisterous fans wanted a top ten finish. He had to be realistic, however, and look at what Tubby had left him.

A bunch of utility players who liked to showboat. Now he knew he could, if he worked hard enough, whip them into solid players. Curbing the showboating would be another thing entirely. He would have to bring in a hardcore recruiting staff. Tubby hadn't brought in a single All-American in the nine years he'd been there. He loved and respected Tubby, but Smith just hadn't been the right fit at Kentucky, and he had to decide if he was.

"Baby, it's up to you. I'll go wherever you go," Rhiannon had told him.

"You understand, you'll be under the same microscope that I'm going to be. You'll be just as famous and the fans will demand just as much from you as they do from me."

"I'm from Kentucky. My father was a coach for Paul Dunbar High. My brother played for him and went on to play Division II ball. Our lives revolved around the sport. I'm not Joanne Pitino. I understand how it'll be."

"She thought she knew how it was going to be too. Her dates consisted of running down balls while Rick shot baskets when they were in high school."

She had kissed him then.

"Do what you have to do Nick, and I'll be right beside you."

So now, he stood before the alumni of UK and a horde of local and national press watching his every move. Mitch Barnhart stood in front of him introducing him as the new head coach of the University Kentucky Wildcats. If it was possible he was more nervous than when he'd been coaching Florida in the NCAA title game. And up until now that had been his biggest moment to shine. Now that he was at Kentucky it was a whole new ball game.

"And it is my pleasure to introduce to you, the new head coach of the Kentucky Wildcats, Nick Ruiz."

A wild applause rang in his ears and a wide grin

involuntarily came up on his face. He was home. This was right. It was his destiny.

***

Kiara wasn't as heavy as he'd thought, and by the time he was carrying her over the threshold of his home they were both cracking up and humming the wedding march. She had a great laugh, and it tickled his ears. It made him laugh even harder.

"Stop it," she gasped, "it hurts."

"All right," he said lying her down on the couch in his living room.

For a split second they stopped. Looked at each other, then burst out laughing again.

"You're killing me," she said in between gales of laughter.

"Then stop making me laugh," he responded.

"Me?" she said continuing to laugh uncontrollably, "you started it."

"Yes you. You and you're dirty jokes. Fifteen minutes late. I'm going to have to keep an eye on you."

"Maybe. But I'll definitely have to keep an eye on you. What do you want me to do when you have, ahhum, have company?"

He'd been having such a good time with Kiara he hadn't thought about that.

"We'll worry about that when the time comes. For now I'm going to go get your cat and your things from the truck."

He started for the door. Before he could get out Kiara stopped him with her voice.

"Thanks, for everything, you know. Not many people would just step into a void like that."

He turned around, "You need to know that there are good people in this world. I'm going to introduce you to some before your stay with me is over."

"Do you know my friend Crista?"

"You mentioned her when you woke up. Is she a friend I can get in touch with for you?"

"I wish."

"Did you have a falling out with her or something?"

"More like something. She died about a year ago. I miss her very, very much."

"I didn't mean to bring you down."

"You didn't," she said pausing, "now go get my kitty."

"All right, all right, I still can't you named an orange tabby after the wrestler Chyna."

"It was the only name Crista and I could agree on."

"What was that I was saying. Oh, that's right, ketchup please. Goes quite nicely with that foot in my mouth."

"You don't have to walk on eggshells around me. Just go get my things please. I'm sure Chyna's freaking out right about now."

Holding up his hands, Adam smiled, and laughed, "Going, going."

As he walked out the door, Kiara tried to wrap her head around the past week's events. Starting with when she was fired. Shitty day. Even if you did include the apology and night of basketball from a very good looking ex-manager. Justine's experience, the flowers from Adam, fly kicking Horatio had been most satisfying, but it brought on a wave a memories and Adam had reached out to her. He'd left with the promise they would watch the title game. And he'd kept his promise. And Junior. He'd hunted her down. She'd almost gotten away from him. If only she hadn't tripped. If only he'd never touched her as a kid. The urge to vomit almost overwhelmed her.

"Hey, are you okay?"

She forced a smile to her lips.

"I'm fine."

Adam set her things down and locked the door behind him. She had to force herself to relax.

He opened the pet carrier and Chyna ran straight to Kiara. She kissed her and stroked her coat. She was glad to see her pet. She had missed her. Up until now she'd been Kiara's only companion over the last year. Together they had grieved Crista's loss.

"I would love for a woman to treat me the way you're treating that cat."

"Oh come on Adam, don't tell me you have a shortage of women waiting to fill that role."

He smiled, "I guess not. But I don't exactly put up a sign that I'm a relationship kind of guy."

"You don't say?" she said, forcing a grin back up. Thoughts of Junior and Crista plaguing her mind.

"You know, I can tell when someone's putting on an act and when they're really okay. And Kiara, you are far from okay. With the week you've had...I wouldn't be okay either."

Chyna purred loudly in her lap. She didn't want to cry. But he was helping her, he deserved to know at least something about what he was up against.

"Sit down. I don't know how much I'll be to tell you. But you need to know as much as I can bare to tell you."

"Kiara..."

"Please, while I still have the nerve to do it, sit down."

Adam swallowed hard and gingerly lifted her legs and joined her on the couch. Resting his hand at her thigh he squeezed it.

"Only what you can. I won't be like the others in your life. I won't allow it."

Taking a deep breath she looked at Adam and began, "It all started around the time I was five..."

Chapter Six

It was sunny, blue skies, so clear there didn't seem to be a cloud in sight. And it was her birthday. She was five. F-I-V-E, five. She couldn't wait for her party to start, she actually got to have friends from school over this year. Even if her family was a little different. But her mom had promised not to smoke any of her 'special' cigarettes before her party. She promised she wouldn't do anything until after her birthday was over.

"Ki, Natasha's here," her uncle Junior called.

She didn't like her uncle Junior. He was gross and scary. He looked normal. About her father's height with her mother's green eyes and tight lips. But there was something about him that wasn't quite right. And even now, there was a deception in his voice that she didn't quite like.

She tried to avoid him. Even when her mother forced her to sit in his lap, or give him a hug she did her best to make it clear that she wanted no part of him.

He called to her again. Only this time his voice was closer. A warm breeze rustled her shorts and tank top. Her heart started to beat a little quicker. Natasha was most definitely not there. She had to hide. The tree house. Yeah, the tree house. She shimmied up the ladder and waited for the danger to pass.

Junior skulked around the corner. Kiara was just back here, he'd seen her go around the corner. His sister was inside getting high. So much for promises. He wanted to wish his niece a happy birthday. Everyone around her was always failing her. He didn't want fail her too, he loved her. Even if she was afraid of him. He didn't want her to be afraid of him. He wanted her to love him. He wanted to show her how much he loved her.

"Ki," he called, "it's just me. I think Natasha is here. I heard a car pull up in the driveway."

Kiara wanted to throw up. She sat curled in a ball in the far corner, praying that he would just leave. But then she heard it, his steps coming closer, rubber scraping against wood. She began to shake. When he popped his head into the tree house she began to wet herself. Then she started to cry.

Hoisting himself up he whispered, "You don't have to be scared. It's just your Uncle Junior. I'm not going to hurt you. I haven't hurt you before now have I?"

He rose to his feet and walked over to her, hovering over her, reaching down and touching her face.

"Now stand up Ki, I want to show you how much you deserve to be loved."

"No," she said, her voice shaking.

A flash of anger went through him.

"What?"

"No."

He wrapped his fist up in her hair and pulled her up to her

feet.

"You will not say no to me, understand?"

"No," her voice virtually disappeared.

He struck her hard across the face, leaving a fast rising welp on her face.

"I love you, Ki, and by God, you're going to love me," he said unbuckling his jeans and shoving them down.

She opened her mouth to scream but he clamped it shut with his hand.

"Now get down on your knees and show me how much you love me."

He forced her to her knees, and when he shoved his thing into her mouth she started to gag.

"That's right baby girl. That's right. Suck me. Suck me hard."

She broke down in tears, retching with each thrust into her mouth. She wanted to make it stop. She wanted him to disappear. She wanted to die.

***

Adam didn't know what to say. It had been a long time since

he'd had a friendship with member of the opposite sex. And even then not one of them had told him a story like the one he had just heard. It explained a lot about Kiara. And about the disgusting woman who had called herself Kiara's mother. But he had to say something, she wasn't saying anything, and she'd been unable to make eye contact with him the entire time she'd been telling him the story. He cleared his throat.

"So what happened afterwards?"

She looked up with a smile, tears glistening in her eyes.

"Natasha didn't come over. My mom and her friends ate the birthday cake because they got high, and I locked the door to my bedroom and didn't sleep a wink. So, are you ready to send me back to my apartment so that I can get a nurse's aide and I can let you off the hook?"

"God no. I like you. And if anyone comes near you ever again, they're going to pay."

She laughed. Are you my platonic knight in shining armor?"

"I certainly something. Seeing you lying there in the hospital. It hurt me. So I sat there and watched you sleep. And I watched that door. And I made sure that only Justine made her way in. When they didn't think you were going to make it I read UK articles. About Nick Ruiz and how he was being a dick in he way he was handling things. But also how he could be the second coming of Rick Pitino."

"Ain't nobody the second coming of Rick Pitino. I don't care how many national championships he's got. If Rick had stayed he'd have just as many as Ruiz, if not more. But Pitino's at Louisville now, with the potential to do there what he did at Kentucky. Ruiz is still the protégé."

He found himself gazing at Kiara. She smiled again. This time without the tears.

"What?"

"Just you. No matter how bad things are, it seems like basketball is your universal cure."

"It's been my touchstone for a long time. There are other things I like to do, but I've bled blue for since as long as you can remember."

"Was your family into it?"

"My dad was. That's what they tell me anyway."

"Oh, I'm sorry, I didn't know."

"No one does. Crista knew. Crista knew just about everything."

"Who did your dad like?"

"The Wildcats of course."

"What happened to your dad? If it's okay to ask."

"You're my friend, you can ask me anything you want. My dad was a marine during the Vietnam War. When he came back he wasn't the same man who left. I know very little about him. Anything he left behind got picked over by his relatives. And I guess that's when mom fell apart. I was about three when it happened. One night he just shot himself in the head. My mom doesn't talk about him and his family has nothing to do with us. But then, why would they? Look at us. A bunch of inbred, incestuous, losers."

A sense of protection boiled up in him as he clasped her hand in his.

"You are not an inbred loser, and what happened to you is not your fault."

"That's nice of you to say, but I already know it wasn't my fault."

"Do you? Really?"

She flinched.

"It's not."

"Listen, I don't want to talk about my past. I don't really want to talk about my present. Basketball is much more fun and much easier."

Adam leaned into her and caressed her cheek.

"You are not damaged goods. You're an attractive woman with a lot to offer this world."

"You talk like a girl."

"I'm serious."

"Look at me. Look at me and say it again and mean it. Guys like I like, do not go for women like me."

He stayed close, she tried not to betray how she was feeling with her eyes or her face. She was terrified at being so close to a man. But Adam wasn't only hot, but he'd proven himself to be a good friend under dire circumstances when he didn't have to, and he loved basketball, UK basketball, almost as much as she did. He was beautiful.

"And what kind of woman are you?"

"Fat."

He was taken aback. He found her to be a desirable woman. He was about to say so when he thought back to their meeting at Damon's not that long ago. He'd found her 'chunky'.

"I like the way you look."

"Ha ha, very funny."

He ran his fingers through her hair.

"I wasn't being funny."

"All right, now you're just being cruel."

He brought her mouth close to his.

"I don't joke around when it comes to this. Close your eyes, Kiara. I promise, this time, it's not going to hurt."

Everything in her screamed you'll be sorry, she didn't care. She closed her eyes and waited.

She was sweet, and when he kissed her, tender. If he had expected her not to kiss him back he wouldn't have done it. Even though it took a little coaxing she did and when she slid her arms around his neck he pulled her body to his and let the sweetness go on and on until their lips parted. He pressed his forehead to hers and smiled.

"I like you, Kiara, I like you a whole, whole lot."

She pressed her palms to his face and smiled.

"I like you too, you know."

Adam kissed her forehead, and pulled her close, holding her in his arms. He liked her. He liked her a whole, whole, lot.

* * *

Meeting with the boys had been a challenge, some of them missed their old coach, some of them wanted to transfer. And the others? Others were so demoralized by a fanbase that didn't believe in them and a coach who'd abandoned them in spirit long ago. Nick had quite the job before him, and the way the press was coming at him for his DUI record was unpleasant too, he hadn't really counted on that, that had caught him off guard. And the way the spotlight was starting to blister down on him, he had to admit, it was a bit overwhelming. Nothing at Florida could have prepared him for the highest profile job in collegiate sports period. Even if he had won back to back national titles. As much as that had counted in getting him the job, it was nothing now that he had it.

"Honey?" Rhiannon called from their Florida kitchen, "Are you sure you've made the right decision?"

He smiled, taking a seat on his hotel room bed in Kentucky. "I'm positive honey."

"You never got this much attention down here, not even this year until they started scouting you for that position up there."

"I thought you said you could handle this."

"I can, Nick, I just want to handle it with you, not behind you."

"Do you want to fly up here and help me look for a house?"

She certainly did not want to stay down in Florida where the anti-Ruiz sentiment was at an all time high. But flying was not an option.

"You know I can't."

"Well, then sit tight and I'll be home in a few days."

"I don't like this."

"Well you better get used to it, you're the one who said you would do this if I really wanted it."

"I lied."

"I've signed a contract, it's too late for that kind of bullshit now."

She steamed. Nick was right. The decision had been made. The only right she had now was to go along for the ride.

"I'll give it until the baby's born. If I still don't like it you have to consider leaving."

Nick's heart fell. He loved his wife. He loved his coming child. But he had been dreaming of coaching UK ball all his life. He hoped it did not come down to his family and his job, because he had a sickening feeling in the pit of his stomach about who would win and he knew in his heart of hearts Rhiannon would hate him for it. And he did not want Rhiannon to hate him for it.

"Sure honey, whatever you say."

"Now that's the man I married."

No it wasn't. And he knew it. And she was fooling herself if she didn't know it.

***

It was quiet in the house as Kiara and Adam laid in the livingroom of Adam's home. And Adam hadn't shared his home with anyone in a long time. He thought of Layla. Layla had been perfect. Or so he'd thought.

Five foot three, long blonde hair and crystal blue eyes. And a body straight out of mythology. But she hadn't an ounce of courage or the strength possessed by the woman who now lay in his arms.

Where Kiara was like a heroine from a meaty novel, Layla was a picture from a fashion magazine; flat, two dimensional, and self obsessed. He knew why he had taken her into his life. He was shallow. But Kiara was different. She had the heart of a survivor and she'd come into his life at a time when he thought life just wasn't worth living anymore. Life had begun to take on a dry and tasteless air and his dreams of sports journalism had looked like a hopeless dream drifting out to sea. But with one kiss, life was starting to taste sweet again.

He kissed the top of her head. She stiffened, then snuggled in close again. He would get justice for her. If it was the last thing he did.

Chapter Seven

Justine came baring alcohol and steaks for a cook out. Was this two friends she had? Lynn was with her, so did that make three? Three friends. Now that was sweet.

"Okay, in celebration of your last day of physical therapy, I think you should meet Helen and Michael."

"Who's Helen and Michael?"

Adam grinned. "Mom and Dad."

"Say what?"

Justine and Lynn started laughing from the kitchen.

"Mom and Dad, they're dying to meet you."

"What, exactly, have you told them about me?"

Leaning over her on the couch he gave a short kiss.

"Nothing but good things I assure you."

"Do they even know I'm basically living here?"

He grinned again.

"Of course they do. And they know we're not sleeping together, if that's what you're worried about."

She shoved him as hard as she could.

"No, I'm not worried about that. I'm worried that they'll think I'm mooching off of you."

82

"My family doesn't think like that. Relax. Just be yourself.
It hasn't failed you up to this point, why should it now?"

"I think all you have to do is look at my and Crista's
respective families and you'll see where that doesn't work."

Justine and Lynn walked into the livingroom and sat down on
the loveseat.

"We like you. Doesn't that count."

"And I like you. I would hope that counted for something as
well."

"I think the real problem is I don't like me, and I haven't
since...never mind. I refuse to be a downer on what could be a
really nice dinner party."

She reached up and laced Adam's fingers in hers.

"Sit, the coals are still heating up. Besides, it's nice to
have friends."

A knock at the door caused him to kiss the top of her hand
and call out, "It's open."

An older couple in their mid-sixties appeared with a
tupperware bowl and pie pan in hand. The woman was petite, her
hair brown turning gray, and the man was a lot like Adam, tall,

broad shouldered, and for his age, a killer body.

"Mom, I told you that you didn't have to bring anything, that this was on me."

"Oh honey, how sweet. I always bring something. Now tell me, who are these sweet ladies?"

Helen set off her alarm. This was not some sweet lady who could be won over easily.

"This is Justine, and her partner, Lynn," closing the door behind his parents, Adam took the food from his mom and smiled broadly, setting the food down on the coffee table he said, "And this is the woman I've been telling you so much about. Mom, Dad, this Kiara."

Michael smiled just as broadly and joined them and took her hand much the same way Adam had.

"It's a pleasure, Kiara. I can see why Adam has taken to you so quickly."

Helen cleared her throat.

"Yes, it's clear that our son has a very big heart. Some people have the habit of taking advantage of that."

"Helen."

"Mom."

Both father and son chided in unison.

"Look, I'd be suspicious of a fast connection, especially the kind of one I've made with your son Mrs. Matthews. But I promise you, I'm not out to get him, use him, or drag him down."

Helen gave her a how sweet, you poor, poor, child look. Instead of hurting her feelings it made her mad.

"Dear, you may not mean to do those things, but in my experience that's exactly what girls like you do."

"Helen!" Michael and Adam's voices boomed.

"No, that's all right. Let her say what she's got to say. Because when she's finished I've got plenty to say to her."

"See Adam. I told you she had no sense of respect."

"You know Mr. Matthews. You seem like a real nice man, and under other circumstances I bet your wife is a real nice woman. But I've paid my dues with my life and I really like your son and that isn't about to change anytime in the near future."

Adam never thought he'd be put in a situation like this in his life. But he cared about Kiara, enough to risk his mother's wrath. Because if truth be told, his mother never liked any of the women he brought around. And Kiara. Kiara had gotten up and mixed it up with his mother. She was a good eleven years his junior and she'd still down. Hell, it was the rare occasion that even he did it. Taking Kiara's hand he helped her to her feet.

"I like her, Mom, and that's just that. Now why don't you give Kiara a hug, I'll put the food out and you ladies sit and chat while us men grill the meat."

Kiara took a deep breath. It wasn't in her nature to give second chances. Any hope of that had been burned out of her when Crista passed and her family had shut her out. But today was a new day. And after everything Adam had done for her over the last few months she was willing to extend the olive branch for his sake.

"If you don't mind Helen, my ankles are still a little iffy, I don't mind doing it if you're not."

Helen wanted to stay mad. She really wanted to. But the girl was being so accommodating it was difficult to stay that way. With a begrudging heart she walked over to Kiara and wrapped her arms around her.

"I'm only doing this for Adam."

Kiara laughed. It was infectious.

"How funny, that's what I was just thinking, Helen."

Kiara felt Adam's large, warm, hand on her shoulder, and his mouth against her ear.

"Thank you, things could've gotten really ugly."

Kiara turned around in his arms and she kissed him with a short, sweet, kiss.

"I suppose. But having you for a son makes her a lucky mom, and having you in my life just makes me lucky period."

Adam gazed down at her and smiled. If he played his cards right he would be a very lucky man. Period.

* * *

The summer breeze was sweet and cool with the smell of grilled meats on the air. His Dad sat in a lawn chair nursing a Bud Ice while he tended the grill.

"So tell me, Adam, do you really like this girl?"

"Yes, Dad. I wouldn't have invited you and mom over if I didn't."

"After what you told us you can't blame your mother for how she acted."

"Mom's an adult Dad. She's responsible for her actions."

"Yeah, but you have to admit Son, Kiara comes with a lot of baggage."

"We all come with a lot of baggage, Dad. She's just had more than her fair share of hard knocks. Doesn't mean she isn't a good person."

"I'm sure she's a great person. Does that mean you have to choose to be around her?"

"Do we have to have this conversation, Dad? I'm not a kid anymore."

"I know. That's what I'm worried about. You're forty-two years old. In your youth maybe I would've looked the other way. But you are not in your youth anymore."

"But I am old enough to know a disaster on wheels when I see one. And Kiara is not a disaster, she's a blessing."

"I don't know. You've never been like this over a girl before."

"And what's that supposed to mean?"

"So open, so...affectionate. Even with Layla, I think you were always careful to keep your indiscretions away from your mother and me."

Adam closed his eyes and took deep, measured, breaths. Michael seemed to sense he had stepped over some invisible line because he started back pedaling immediately.

"I'm sorry Adam, I didn't mean for it to sound so bad. I'm just concerned for you."

"How? She treats me like I matter. She believes in me. She likes me Dad. And I like her. And if you and Mom can't deal with that then you can both leave. Now."

"Now calm down, calm down, there's no need to get in an uproar."

"Other than the fact you just called my girlfriend an 'indiscretion' I suppose we're fine. No wonder she has such a chip on her shoulder when it comes to meeting strangers. They assume things without ever getting to know her. I'm embarrassed to say I was one of them. But you are not going to make her uncomfortable in my home."

"Have you slept with the girl?"

"No."

"Are you sure about that? Because you're acting like a

virgin who just got his first taste of the opposite sex."

"Watch your mouth old man, you are treading on some thin ice."

"Your mother and I just want what's best for you, you have to understand."

"What I understand is that I care about Kiara a great deal and that you're not respecting any of my choices. Which is ironic, because as long as I'm some burnt out failed sports journalist you're fine with my choices. As soon as I try to put my life in order you and Mom have problems with it."

"She was abused, she sees a psychiatrist for Godssake."

"And up until two or three months ago I slept with everything that walked and broke a lot of hearts along the way. That and I'm a really lousy restaurant manager."

"You're a good looking guy, you can write as good as the next Sports Illustrated guy."

"So what would I want with a girl like Kiara."

"Well, yeah Son. I guess that's what I'm asking."

"First. She's smart. Second. She's funny. And third, when she talks UK basketball she lights up from the inside out and she just shines with this beauty, the kind of beauty I've never seen before on woman. Not even on Mom. This kind of beauty is hard fought, hard won, and much, much deserved. It makes me want to take her in my arms kiss her and hold her, and protect her, and make love to her. She's worth it Dad. And if I get any indication of you and Mom rejecting her, making her feel like an 'indiscretion' it will be a long, long time, if ever, you talk to me again."

The meat sizzled on the grill and Michael could not believe his ears. It had taken forty-two years, but his son had grown up.

"All right, Son. If she's what you want, your mother and I will support you. But I have to warn you, if there's even a hint of unhappiness, then we're coming in, loaded for bear."

"Just understand, you hurt her, you hurt me. And I'm coming in, loaded for much more bear than you could ever wrap your head around."

***

Night had come and everyone had gone home. Leaving only Kiara and Adam in the house. Adam stood out on the porch looking up at the stars. Why on earth were his parents making such asses

out of themselves. They had never been like this with Layla.
Layla.

Layla who had, up until now, been the only woman to hold his
interest for more than a nano second. Layla, who'd been the
spitting image of a woman who he was supposed to bring home. His
parents had loved her. Taken her in. Made her one of the family.
And you talk about a woman with a past, where she was from she'd
apparently gotten around and then some. It was many a night when
the phone would ring with some man begging her to come back to
them. She'd brushed it off, reassuring him that he was the only
one she wanted. And he'd believed her. Idiot that he was. His
cock and heart crossed signals and he'd proposed to her. Much
like on a night like tonight.

A warm summer night with a cool breeze, and the stars out
shining bright. Thoughts of Layla pained him, even now, but for a
different reason. His parents had crucified him and his choice of
woman. Kiara had done nothing wrong other than survive and be the
anti-thesis of the type of girl he brought them. When he did
bring them around.

Kiara's words from a few months ago haunted him now. *Girls like me, don't get guys like you*. She was smart. She was funny. And she was passionate about UK basketball to the point of ecstasy. And as she had a beauty about her he couldn't put into words, a strength that many did not see. Not even her. But he knew what she was saying with those words. That small, rounded, girls didn't often get the strapping handsome guy. Well for the last few months they had gown close. Closer than close, and things had turned romantic for them. And even though he'd been close minded at their first meeting, he wasn't now.

Soft strains of piano floated out onto the porch and tickled his ears. His parents may have left early, but Justine and Lynn had stayed and the evening had turned out wonderful. There had been laughter and smiles. And cuddling. He loved the way Kiara felt in his arms. Soft, curvy, and full, she had leaned all they way back against his chest. She made him hard with each giggle or laugh and he squeezed her closer to ease the growing ache in his cock.

The piano music stopped and he heard footsteps approached the door. She didn't come out.

"How long are you going to stand there and wait for them to

come back?"

"Wait for who to come back?

"Your parents."

He turned around with a puzzled look on his face.

"Is that what you think I'm doing out here?"

"What else would you be doing?"

"Thinking about you. About us."

She struggled to keep a smile from turning her mouth upward.

"What were you thinking?"

"A lot of things. Why don't you come out here and find out?"

"Why don't you make me?" she said smiling slyly.

"You're still on crutches."

"I can still beat you to the office."

"You better start now, because I'm not waiting any longer."

He laughed as he watched her hop towards the office, wobble and fall to the ground laughing hysterically. He moved in slow, methodical, steps, allowing the door to shut behind him. He locked it, but did not shut the main door. Instead he stalked Kiara as if she were his prey. And was hungry for her. Very, very hungry for her.

As she gasped for breath laughing, a wicked grin flickered across his face. He had been a good boy for months now, and his heart had held him in check. But she was so flushed, and her laughter so great, she was beautiful and lit up from the inside out, and he wanted more than just the taste of her mouth to satisfy him. He wanted to prove to her that yes, girls like her, could always get someone like him.

Chapter Eight

He was on his knees tickling her, and she was gasping for air. He was tickling her so much it almost hurt.

"Say it Kiara."

"Say what?"

"Say what you've been wanting to say all week, but hadn't the nerve to."

"What are you talking about?"

Adam sat back on his heels and lay down on the floor next to her. He propped himself up on his elbow, gazing down at her. She stuck her lower lip out in a mock pout. He ran his thumb over it and she opened her mouth, and brought her hands up to his, taking it in. Licking it, suckling it, before allowing him to draw it out. He sucked in his breath. This was not the way it was supposed to go.

"Hey, did I step over a line or read the signals wrong?"

"Oh no baby, you read the signals right. It's just that I expected to be the one doing the seducing."

"Trust me, that ship sailed a long time ago. When I woke up and you were sitting in the hospital with me, I think I was in love from that moment on."

"So you think I can't do anything to top that?"

"Keeping a bedside vigil is a hard act top. No one's ever done anything like for me before. It's like something out of a story book."

"So am I better than a storybook?"

"You may be human, but you are pretty damn close," she said, smiling up at him and running her fingers through his hair, "you know you oughtta be shot for having as good a head of hair as you do."

"Now is that any way to talk to your storybook boyfriend?"

Laughing, she playfully shoved his head away.

"You're bad."

"Maybe," he said rolling on top of her, "but I promise you I'm a real good man."

She gasped, "You're going to crush me."

A cool breeze swept through the room. The smell of honeysuckles and violets hung lightly on the air.

"Do you like me, Kiara?"

"What are you talking about? Of course I like you, Adam. Why would you even ask me that?"

"Well," he said planting soft, lingering, kisses at her neck, "my parents weren't exactly welcoming to you."

Taking his face in her hands she smiled, a bit of sadness and weariness in her eyes.

"I have faced much tougher opponents than your mom and dad. If you stand by me they strike me as the kind of people who'll eventually come around."

"And here I thought I would be comforting you."

"Hardly, I had a great time with Justine and Lynn. And now I'm rolling around on te floor with you, what more could I ask for?"

Taking her hand he kissed her palm, his tongue darting out and tasting her skin. He eased from her some and placed his thigh between her legs. The sound of her moan pleased him, making his cock so hard it hurt.

"You're going to be the death of me, baby."

His words made her heart swell as much as his thigh made her ache between her legs.

"Say it again."

"Say what?" he grinned down at her, pressing his leg into her, eliciting another moan and shallow breathing.

"Baby, call me baby."

Running his hand up her t-shirt he found her bra-less. It was his turn to moan at the feel of her soft flesh in his roughened palm. When he found her nipple he stroked it gently into a hardened peak until he felt her hips gyrating against his thigh.

"You like that baby? I think you'll like this even more."

Pushing her shirt up he took her breast in his mouth and listened as she groaned, clasping his head close to her chest, moving her hips ever so sweetly against his leg.

Her body pulsed with her senses fully engaged. A man's touch had never electrified her so. Had never made her feel so alive. Made her feel so sexy. Made her feel so...good.

His mouth made her breast his playground, suckling it hard

then soft, then fast and then slow. His tongue danced around her skin, licking her, laving her, while his teeth nipped at her skin until he caught her nipple between both rows of them.

"Oh God," she gasped.

He did not let up. His lips moved like a well conducted orchestra while he snaked his free hand up to fondle her other breast. Her body arched up against his and squirmed madly to be closer, she wanted more, needed more, demanded more. And in her mixture of innocence and wanton abandon, she was sure he craved her touch and much as she did his.

When he hands moved up his back, against his skin he thought he might lose it. Releasing her breasts a disappointed moan reached his ears. He captured her earlobe between his teeth then whispered in her ear, "There's more where that came from Kiara. And it's more fun than that."

"Promise?"

Lifting his thigh, he rubbed her up and down with it.

"Do you trust me?"

Her hips were beginning to move faster, he kissed her savagely, passionately, plunging his tongue into her mouth and

taking from her everything she offered up, including her own
tongue she used to stroke his. He shuddered with each touch.
When their mouths parted he gazed down at her. Her cheeks were
flushed and her eyes were hooded. He continued to rub his leg
against her sex as she continued to move with him. She was so
beautiful. He should tell her so. Before he could she cut him off
at the pass.

"Take off your shirt," her command was soft and husky. And
sexy.

"Only if you take yours off first."

Hers was quickly discarded with, but as she watched him
stretch and remove his her heart hammered in chest making it hard
to breath. He was Michelangelo's David reborn. His stomach was
ripped and his was chest solid. She reached out and touched him.
She tried not to close her eyes as he continued to move against
her but she could feel herself starting to climax. As he could
sense this he dipped down and began to caress one of her breasts
while suckling at the other. Her orgasm crashed down all over her
making her fuck his leg hard and fast. No longer a slave to a
gentle rhythm she thrashed around in the wave. Through clenched

teeth she hissed, "Harder, faster, more."

He was relentless in his fucking of her. He wanted to make her scream. Scream with pleasure. Scream in ecstasy. Scream his name. So he rode her hard like she demanded. Faster like she wanted. More, like she desired. Like he desired.

Suddenly she cried out his name, but it wasn't in ecstasy, it was in terror. He froze and rolled off of her. The moment shattered. He looked around the house then at the door. His heart was racing as he tried to get his bearings. She was crying, and there was fear and shame in those tears. He thought of her past. He thought of her family.

"I'm sorry," she sobbed choking back tears, "it's not you. It's me. All me."

He looked down at her. Her body so beautiful even as she tried to cover it by turning away from him. He raised her and took her into his embrace.

"You've done nothing wrong. Understand. Nothing at all."

She wanted to lean into him. Tell him she was okay, that she could still make him come. But she couldn't. The orgasm she'd just experienced had made her feel alive and good in the presence of a man. But like in previous relationships her demons had come out and gotten the best of her.

"Listen, if you want me to go I'd understand. Plenty of other boyfriends have taken me up on the offer."

"I'm not other boyfriends. I'm the storybook. Remember?"

"I can tell you're frustrated."

"I'm only human. You're a beautiful woman who kissed me, and put her hands on me in a very intimate way, of course I'm a little frustrated. But I'm not mad. And I'm not leaving you, and if I have anything to say about it, you are not leaving me. So don't cry baby. I'm here for you, and we'll take this as fast, or as slow as you want to," he turned her face up to meet his gaze, and grinned a goofy grin, "I just prefer faster."

She reached up and drew him down into a slow, sensual kiss. Hen she pulled back she said, "I know I shouldn't say this, but I love you Adam Paul Matthews. I love you with all my heart."

Her words shocked him. Not in a bad way. They just surprised him and left him speechless.

"I know you're not ready to say it to me. But I couldn't hold it in any longer. I love you Adam. And I think I always will."

It was his turn to kiss her. When they stopped he whispered
in her ear.

"I love you, Kiara Jackson. And I've loved you since you
opened your eyes at the hospital. I don't know why you were put
in my path, but I'm going to love you until the day I die."

They kissed again, only this time they laid back down with
Kiara on top, straddling him, holding each other's hands. His
cock was hard against her sex and it felt good to be there. She
was nervous. Nervous that she would freak out again. But she
wanted to do this. For him. For her. For them. She began to rock
and undulate her body to his. When he groaned it made her feel
good.

"Oh baby, just keep on doing what your doing."

It felt so good as she rode him slow and gentle allowing
herself the space she needed to make him come and not freak out
again.

"Look at me, Kiara. As long as you're with me, no one can
hurt you. No boogeyman, no demons, not anybody, understand?"

She rocked like a she rode a mechanical bull. Back and

forth, back and forth until she felt her own climax beginning all over again, she felt the panic begin to rise. Adam reached up and touched her face.

"Stay focused. Look at me. It's Adam. I love you. Just remember that," he groaned. He wanted to be buried inside of her, feel her hot and wet and clinging to him. But this was good. She knew how to move to make him feel fantastic. She was beginning to rock a little bit faster, a little bit harder. If she didn't watch it she was going to make him come before she had a chance to. He watched, her body moving, undulating, as if she were giving him a private show. She smiled at him and it reached her eyes. The look said I love you. Then her back arched and she held back no longer. She cried out his name. But this time it was with pleasure. She said it again. And it made him come. She said it again and she collapsed to him.

Breathing hard, their bodies hot and sweaty, they said nothing. She loved him. He loved her. They kissed as he wrapped his strong arms around her.

"Promise me you'll never leave me," he said, breaking the silence.

"Shouldn't I be asking you that question?"

"Just promise. If you're scared, you'll come to me, and that you won't run away."

Kissing him and resting her chin on his chest. She smiled.

"I promise."

Bunching her hair up in his hands he kissed her as if he were a thirsty man who'd just found water.

"I love you, Kiara."

"I love you, Adam Paul."

And he always would love her. He hoped she could feel that.

She would always love him, and she would prove to him that she deserved every drop of faith he was investing in her.

***

It was late. Adam had shut all the windows and locked up for the night. The air conditioner was on now and the house freezing. But she liked it that way. The air in her apartment was never working and she had a delinquent landlady to boot. So freezing temperatures were good, besides it gave her a good excuse to snuggle under the covers with Adam while watching a tape of the 1998 NCAA Regional Final of UK versus Duke. With the lights turned off it was like watching the best movie titled, 'The Comeback Cats'.

"You know, I think my favorite part is when Scott Padgett nails a three pointer to put the 'Cats up with just a few seconds left to go."

"This was when everybody loved Tubby."

"That was when Tubby was winning. What do you say to a coach who has a 70% winning percentage, but can't seem to recruit. I'm sure he's a great guy, and he is a great coach, he just didn't fit at UK."

"What do you think of Nick Ruiz?"

"I'm sure Florida wants to burn him at the stake, but I'm glad he came here. Although he strikes me as the kind of guy who wants to move up, so once he works his magic at UK I'm sure he'll be looking to go to the pros."

"I've got to ask you something."

"Okay."

"Actually, it's two somethings."

"Just out with it."

"First, I'm forty-two. You're thirty-one. What is your life

ambition, and do you think it's too late for me to fulfill mine?"

"My ambition, my secret desire, has always been to write and play concert piano. But I don't own a piano, and I haven't had many lessons, what you heard earlier was the extent of my knowledge. And I don't think it's ever too late for someone to grab a hold of their dreams."

"You should be proud of that."

"Proud of what?"

"That your hope hasn't been crushed by what's happened to you."

"You have to hope. If you don't have hope, what else do you have? I thought you had a second question."

"I did," he said smiling down at her.

About that time Cameron Mills put up the three that tied the game.

"Sweet!" she yelled.

"Pay attention to the man behind the curtain."

"Okay okay. It's just that this game happens to be one of my favorites."

"I want to know if you would like to make your stay here a

more permanent situation."

Her eyes lit up, and she glowed from the inside out. "Yes," she said with tears in her eyes, "yes."

Gathering her up close he kissed her sweetly.

"Then welcome home, Kiara. Welcome home."

Chapter Nine

Nick thought his head might explode from the headache that was pounding in his skull. The hiring of his assistant coaches was going great. But things at home were getting worse. Much worse.

"You and your fucking team. I'm seven months pregnant. With your baby and I can't buy five minutes with you. Five minutes. That's all I'm asking for."

"Those boys are counting on me to make the transition between me and their last coach, whom they loved very much, a smooth one. So excuse me if I've been less than 600% at your beckon call."

Rhiannon was a beautiful woman. Especially at seven months. She glowed. Even in her anger. He only had two real passions in his life. College basketball and his wife. And he didn't have any desire to lose either one of them.

Walking over to her, he tried to smile.

"I know you're mad, and that this is more than what you expected. But try to look at it this way. We're close to your family. When it's time for the baby they won't have to fly anywhere, they'll just have a short drive to the hospital."

"Mad? Is that what you think I am? You leave at six o'clock in the morning to head into the office and look at film and scouting reports. You call parents of potential players and give them all the time they need. You send your recruiters down for the ones who you think will come to UK without question, and you set up flights for yourself for the ones you think need that special touch. You're as crazy as the fans are. Sometimes I think you're married to them and not to me."

He reached out to hold her. She pulled away.

"No, Nick. A hug and a kiss isn't going to make it all better."

"Look around us, Rhiannon. Look at this home. Look at us. You, me, the baby. We have everything we've ever wanted."

"Wrong Nick. You have everything you've ever wanted. I'm a stay at home wife who has to smile and cheer for her husband at every turn. And I'm pregnant. And alone. All the friends I made down in Florida hate me now, because you just had to take the job here. There we could be champions without the fan pressure. Here it's already started."

"What is it that you want, honey? Tell me, and it's yours."

"I want my job as partner at Fredrick, Martin, and Straus back."

"We're not moving back to Florida. We decided that this move was the right one."

"You decided that, Nick."

"No, if I recall correctly you said whatever decision I made you would stand beside me."

Her eyes narrowed.

"Go to Hell, Nick."

"What?" his voice exploded, "it's the truth."

"You knew my career was important to me. Ever since we got here I haven't had the time to look for a new job."

"And you knew what kind of man I was when you married me. Basketball was my passion. Is my passion. And I'm not about to give it up."

"I'm not asking you to, I'm just saying you're not just a coach, you're a husband, and your about to be a father. I need you as much as those 'boys' do, if not more."

Nick sighed. He and Rhiannon had been having this argument over and over lately. He was sick of having it. It was too hard. Of course his job demanded a lot from him. This wasn't Florida, this was fucking UK, the Wildcats of Kentucky, located in the heart of Lexington. He needed her to understand. To be there for him. He knew it wasn't fair, that in some ways it wasn't right, but that was what she signed on for when she said 'I do'. But he could hear Dr. Phil in his head chanting *do you want to be right? Or do you want to be happy?* He wanted to be happy. And right now, happy meant his wife and his job, he had to find a way to balance it.

"Come here, honey," he said taking her in his arms, "you've made a lot of sacrifices for me to make this possible. If you want to work, work. As for friends, I know you, you'll charm everyone you meet, then you'll win them over and decide if they're really worth having as friends."

"And you'll cut back on you're hours when the baby gets here."

A little lie couldn't hurt anyone. It was like when Al Pacino said to Diane Keaton in The Godfather. Just this once, just this once he would answer her question. And just like in the movie, for the marriage's sake, it would have to be a lie.

"For a little while yes, I'll cut back the hours. I want you to be as happy as I am."

She leaned into him, he could feel her breath shallow and uneven against his chest.

"I just wanted you to understand how hard this has been for me, and that I couldn't do it alone."

Stroking her hair, fear gripped his heart, he did not want to choose between his two loves. But if he had to, he would.

"I understand, honey. Don't ever doubt that I do, or that I

love you."

She held on tight. He held on back. UK was the place he'd dreamed of coaching at since Rick brought him there in 1989. He had a home. He had a wife. He had a baby on the way. Life was full, and for the moment good.

***

Adam hadn't called his college roommate in nearly five years. They had both majored in Sports Journalism and set out to conquer the world. Thomas Quentin had conquered the world, his small pieces had landed him the splashy job of contributing editor for Sports Illustrated. Both of them had attended UK, and Thomas had been the lone voice of compassion for his team when scandal hit them in 1988.

Adam had unwittingly given Thomas the inside track on the Rick Pitino story, twice. Some people said he was a fool to talk to Thomas. But for the most part Thomas was a good guy. You just had to watch your leads around him.

"Hi, you've reached Thomas and Eddie, we're not home right now, but if you'll leave your name and number we'll be sure to get right back to you."

Shit. He really needed to talk to Thomas. Thomas and Eddie, how long had he had that dog? He was just as bad about that German Shepherd as Kiara was about her cat, Chyna.

"Tom, it's Adam. I know it's been a while but if you could give me a buzz I have some info you might be interested in. Bye."

As soon as he hung up the phone rang back. Typical Thomas.

"Hey there Adam," came a booming, rich, southern, voice, "what do you have for me?"

"How about, how's it going Adam. Sorry to have lost touch Adam. Don't you believe in pleasantries of any kind?"

"You're such a girl. Now I know you wouldn't have called me if you didn't have something on the line that would be interest to the both of us. Only last time we had a conversation like this I beat you to the punch."

"You did it the last couple of times. And that's why I'm managing an Applebees in Fern Creek, Kentucky and you're working for SI."

Thomas laughed.

"Your time is coming, friend. I can feel it."

"That's what you told me shortly before your article on Rick broke across the Courier Journal's front page."

A chuckle greeted Adam's ears.

"I guess that did happen, huh?"

"You are far, far, from funny, Tom."

"Oh lighten up. Now you said you had something on the line for me."

"I might. But I might want to write the article myself."

"You still chasing that rabbit?"

"Some of us are just late bloomers."

"Well, it's not because you don't have the talent. My ears are open, Adam, speak."

"I have a spin on this whole hoopla surrounding the UK coaching hire situation."

"If it's about their marriage being on the rocks, save it. Everyone querying us is making that pitch."

"It's more about the fans of Kentucky. And the angle is about who is the number one fan of the flagship that calls itself Big Blue Nation."

"Everyone thinks they're the number one fan of something, somewhere. They're called stalkers Adam. Not SI stories, not even penny rag stories. Any sports writer worth their salt will tell you that those type of stories only sell during championship time and even then they're far and few between."

"You disappoint me. You've seem to have forgotten your Kentucky roots. The fans are what makes this sport what it is. Especially the Wildcat fans. And I've found one who transcends the hype. She is a number one fan without being a stalker."

"How can you be sure of this? Selena thought her fan club president was just a dedicated fan. And that bitch was crazy. Do you want to be the one with Nick Ruiz's blood on your hands?"

"Nick Ruiz's blood isn't going to be on my hands."

"How can you be so sure?"

"Because I know the lady."

"You know the lady. From what I remember, you know lots of ladies, Adam."

"It's not like that."

"Then what is it like? Your pitch is boring me, and friend or not, you've got about thirty seconds to make me interested."

"Her name is Kiara Jackson, and she is so obsessed with UK basketball she not only named the new coach before he popped up on the radar, she successfully called thirty out of thirty-five games of the NCAA tournament."

There was silence on the other end of the line.

"How do you know her?"

"She used to work for me at Applebees."

"Are you or have you slept with her?"

"I don't think that's of any real importance."

"I'm going to have to pass. Although up until then you had a pretty good story. I might send one of my boys out to cover the angle."

A rush of anger shot through Adam.

"This is my story goddammit!"

"Then I suggest you write it before your toy up and runs out on you."

"She is not my toy, she is my girlfriend, and you'd do well to keep that in mind when talking about her."

"Maybe you're not fucking her. I change my mind. Run with the story. I have no doubt you can write, here's your chance."

"What if I am sleeping with her?"

"Don't tell me about it. I may be your friend, but I am not

your girlfriend you can gossip and talk with."

The anger subsided. Was he actually going to be published in SI? Only if Kiara agreed to it. It would be her life put on display. Her passion, her pain, her survival. If he did his job right it would be plastered all throughout Sports Illustrated for the readers to see. He had to get her okay. And to be honest, he had no idea if he would get it.

***

She thought about the upcoming trial and wondered if she could take it. Her whole life had been tied up in living the fear, the shame, and the pain of her family that she just wanted to hide and forget about them. This latest attack bothered her more than the others. She'd been free of them for ten whole years. Pulling the eggs out of the fridge, she smiled through the new pain. She had something new to hang her hat on. Adam. And basketball. And sometimes, when he wasn't looking, she played his baby grand piano. Maybe one day she would write music to play on the piano. That made her happy. Not as happy as her friendship with Crista had made her, but then, she doubted anything ever would.

Turning the flame on under the frying pan she started fixing breakfast. He hadn't said as much, but she was practically living there, and even though the meeting with the parents had been something of a disaster he'd stood by her. Much like Crista had. Although, Kiara had to admit, Crista paid a far higher price to be who she was than Adam did to be who he was. Adam was a strong, sexy, beautiful man, who, at home was a far different man than he'd ever been at work.

She poured the mixed egg and cheese mixture into the crumbled up sausage and began to stir. She let a spark of joy shock her system. It felt good, it felt right. When his arms encircled her waist and he buried his face in her hair, her joy must have been all over her face.

"You should smile more often, it lights up your face."

"You say that to all the girls you date."

"I haven't lived with a woman in three years. And before that the women I dated were nothing like you," he said nibbling at her neck.

She switched the flame down on low and turned around in his arms so that she could see him.

"I am so lucky," she said sighing, "and not because a gorgeous guy like you is having anything to do with a girl like me, but because a guy like you hasn't been scared away by a girl like me."

"Really? I thought I was the lucky one," he said, kissing her.

She blushed. She still wasn't used to the intimate way he always kissed her. Like she was his, and he was hers. In a good way. When he kissed her, he washed away the shame her family had so brutally branded her with.

"I love it when you do that. You've given me a shot at the kind of life I never thought I would ever have the desire to have again."

"You sweet talker you. Are you sure you want to be with me, even though I haven't let you passed the pearly gates yet?"

"Kiara, that will come in due time. You have your reasons. And like you said, I'm the storybook, right?"

"I think I should've kept that comment to myself. I've given you a big head."

Brushing his lips over hers he whispered, "More than you can possibly know."

"Tease."

A playful grin turned up the corners of his mouth.

"You'd better check those eggs before you scorch or burn them."

Twirling around she picked up her spatula.

"Oh shit. You come in here and get me all hot and bothered and look what you make do."

He squeezed her behind and nipped at her earlobe.

"Oh there's much more where that came from."

A gasp and moan escaped her lips.

"Do it again."

A broad, toothy grin spread across his face as he cupped her cheeks and repeated the process.

"Did you mean this?"

"Yes."

"Do you want me to do it again?"

"No."

"Why not?"

"Because I'll forget the fact I'm fixing breakfast and I

will burn the eggs."

Backing off he sat down at the table, and stuck out his lower lip, "Oh alright."

Looking over her shoulder she smiled.

"Don't worry, there's much more where that came from."

"Shameless."

"Only with you."

"I know baby."

"You are too, you know."

"What's that?"

"Shameless."

"When it comes to you, hopelessly."

Turning the eggs off she heaped two plates full and set the on the table, then sat down herself.

"What, no biscuits, no juice."

"Fuck."

She started to get up, but Adam quickly stopped her.

"I'm just kidding. I'll get the juice and the bread. You eat."

"I can..."

Kiara couldn't shake the fear she'd had ingrained her from a very young age. That if she did not earn her keep she would be punished. Often severely, and usually, by her mother. Adam was talking, but she was a million miles away.

"Kiara, Kiara," he said, setting her juice down, "Kiara."

Her eyes had gone blank, and her face was as still as stone.

"Kiara!"

She snapped to and her eyes welled up with tears.

"I'm sorry. God I'm sorry. Please don't hit me, please don't leave me. Please..." she cried.

He stood up and walked over to her, bringing her to her feet, and drawing her close.

"You don't have to be sorry, you've done nothing wrong. And if you ever need to know one thing about me it's that I'll never raise hand to you, or leave you. I don't know what the future holds, but I'm here for the duration. Got that?"

She nodded against his chest. He held her tight to him. To lose her was unthinkable.

"Now, come on, let's eat breakfast before it gets cold. I'll even sit closer to make it more romantic."

They sat back down. Neither saying much. Adam had to bring
up the story now. He had a deadline to meet. But he didn't want
to exploit Kiara against her wishes. Her pain was still so raw,
so new that he wanted her blessing before he went ahead with
chasing his dream, and her past.

"Whatever it is that you're wanting to ask me, could you go
ahead and just ask me? I feel like you're staring at me and it's
unnerving me."

"Are you sure you're not a writer? Unnerving?"

"Would you just spit it out?"

"Okay, I've been sitting on this for awhile, but I pitched a
story to SI and they've given me the go ahead to write it."

Her face lit up.

"That's great, that means you could cut back on your time at
that hell hole you call a job."

"Maybe. I have to get permission to write it first."

"I thought you just said SI accepted the pitch?"

He took a deep breath, and touched her face.

"The story is you, Kiara. And your obsession with Kentucky
basketball."

"Go for it. I don't care who knows that kind of stuff."

"The readers are going to want to know about you. You're life. Your ups, your downs, that kind of thing."

She looked like he'd just struck her across the face.

"Please, Kiara, talk to me. Yes, no, go to hell. Anything, just talk."

She felt as if the wind had been knocked out of her. Was she just a story to him, had the last few months just been a seduction to get her to open up? A single tear fell down her cheek.

"Is that why you brought me here? To score a magazine article?"

Now it was his turn to feel stricken.

"No. If you don't want me to do the story I won't. Not if it hurts you. Not if it means losing you."

Her breath slowly returned. If anyone told her story it would have to be Adam. He had the talent to pull it off. He had the talent to keep her shielded even if the press came for her. This was his dream, she was trying to have hers, why couldn't he have his.

"Okay."

"Okay what?"

"Okay, you can do the story. But you have to be my storybook, okay?"

"Okay," he leaned forward and kissed her. He could do that forever. Taste her again and again and it never get old. God he was lucky. "Did I mention how lucky I was."

"Yes. But you can tell me again if you like."

Cradling the back of her head with his large hand he kissed her again. Only this time it was longer, and deeper, and wetter. He could never get enough with just one taste. He could do this forever.

"Adam."

"Yeah."

"Will you come to the trial with me?"

"Everyday."

"And you'll make sure everyone knows what kind of monsters my family are?"

"I promise."

"Okay. And Adam?"

"Yes?"

"I love you."

Chapter Ten

Kiara stood out in the evening air bouncing her basketball and switching stances at intervals before shooting. She repeated this process again and again until the light began to fail her. She had worked up a sweat in the summer breeze. It was warm and a sticky, but the rythm of repeating these plays gave her a sense of control. A sense of calm came over her with each dribble and drive to the basket. She had no vertical, but she jumped like she was some kind of Michael Jordan. Even as the light failed her she continued to mimic the plays of Nick Ruiz's Florida Gators. She

just put the names of UK greats in her head. Issel. Givens.
Mashburn. Pelphry. And Brassow to name a few. She loved them all.
And she loved the game of college basketball. But she was trying
to get things off her mind. The impending trial which made her
sick to think about it.

The prosecutor had been drilling her hard to prep her for
when the defense got a hold of her. It would be nasty it would be
hard, and it would be ugly. Reliving her visit with Crista over
and over again was starting to overshadow why she went to the
cemetery in the first place. But she had to testify, without her
on the stand there would be no case. She didn't know which gave
her more nightmares, the memory of the attack, or testifying to
it and facing down her attacker.

Then there was Adam's shot at glory. She dribbled the ball,
set her feet and launched the ball. Sweet string music from three
point land. She looked down, damn, two points. Her foot was on
the line she'd drawn with a piece of sidewalk chalk. She
retrieved the ball. Adam. His shot at glory. Her fear of looking
like a joke before a nation. What if they saw her as some kind of
hillbilly whore? She knew Adam would never do something like

that, but what if that was all that she was? The fear was enough to choke her and make it hard for her to breathe. She zigged, she zagged, she shot, she missed. Bright lights pulled into the driveway. The car was not Adam's. But it wasn't trashy like any of her relatives. Then her heart squeezed in a painful way. Media. A man got out. A burly chested man, not as tall as Adam, but just as sharp a dresser, approached her with his hand stuck out. She scooped up her ball and headed for the side door to the house.

"You are a skittish one. Please don't leave on my account."

"Get off the property."

"Don't you want to know who I am?"

"You could be the second coming of Jesus Christ himself and I'd still tell you to leave."

"My name is Thomas Quentin and I am the contributing editor for Sports Illustrated. And you are?"

"None of your business."

"Quite the sharp little tongue for such a vulnerable woman."

Kiara's eyes narrowed as she turned her back to 'Thomas Quentin' and started up the steps to her new home. She felt his hand on her shoulder, and heard him say, "Hey, wait a minute..." The rest was lost on her as her survival instinct kicked in and she had his arm in position which left him at her mercy.

"Mr. Quentin, you are not wanted here. And if you insist on making veiled threats I will break your arm, and I will do it in a way that makes it not only painful, but excruciating for you. So I'm going to let go and you're going to leave."

Sweat began to line his brow as he tried to squirm out of the hold she had him in. She held her ground.

"I am going to let go of you now, and you're going to leave peaceably, and not threaten me ever again. Or, like I said, I will break your arm. And that will be the least of your problems."

She suddenly felt the unmistakable jerk of Thomas being pulled free from her grasp and the thud of him being thrown against the wall. She focused, it was Adam, and his face was a mask of fierce anger.

"Who the fuck do you think you are putting your hands on her!"

Utter shock and fear was in Thomas's eyes. Adam was seething with his friend's lapels gathered in his fists.

"Answer me God damn it!"

All Thomas could do was stammer.

"Adam, A-a-dam, it's Thomas. The guy who's giving you a shot. Ease up man. I'm not going to hurt her, I swear. I was just yanking her chain."

"That is not acceptable. Understand?"

"Understood, understood. Now could you please let go of me?"

Adam flung him free and cracked his neck.

"Thomas, this is Kiara. Kiara, this is the guy who cheats me out of stories. Don't say a word to him."

"What kind of welcome is that for your old college buddy who's giving you a shot at the big time?"

"The kind who scares my girlfriend."

A look of disbelief went across Thomas's face.

"Her?"

That one stung.

"Yes her. Now get off of my property."

"Oh come on, I didn't mean anything by it."

"Sure you did," Kiara shot back, "you meant you're with that cow?"

"All I meant was that you're not normally the type of girl I see Adam with."

"No, she's much prettier, much smarter, and much more talented than any of the women I've been with in the past."

"I suppose Kiara is the fan you wanted to profile?"

"Yes. And for that reason you won't be coming in."

"Oh come on, I drove all the way from New York to see you."

"No, you came here to see if I had a lead you could steal for yourself. And now you've disrespected her. Let me write the story on my own Thomas."

"I saw you running plays out here. Impressive. Maybe Adam Paul has a story here after all. Okay, I'll back off, for now. And hon, I didn't mean anything by what I said."

Kiara fought back the lump of anger and hurt in her throat.

"Sure you did. Adam, I'm going inside. If you want to play with your friend all that I ask is that you warn me so that I can make myself scarce."

She disappeared into the house, and Adam turned to Thomas. "I don't know what you said or did to her, but it better not happen again."

"Come on Adam. Whose word are you going to take? Mine or hers."

"I've worked really hard to gain her trust, I am not about to let you fuck that all up."

"Oh, so it's for the story..."

"Fuck you man, it's because I love her. Now back off so I can do my story."

"You know, I saw what she was doing before I drove up. I saw what you were talking about. She is like some kind of savant when it comes to this state's official sport. You're lucky I like you, if it had been someone else who'd manhandled me the way you did they'd be without a job right now."

"That's because you know you started it. Now I've got to go clean up the mess you just made. If you want to do lunch tomorrow at Damon's I'm more than up to it. But for tonight you need to leave."

"All right, all right. Tomorrow, Damon's 12:30PM. We'll talk about sports and more about your pitch."

"Whatever, now go before I sic my woman on you again."

Thomas squirmed.

"Tomorrow."

"Tomorrow, Thomas."

Thomas waved before walking to his brand new Cadillac. Adam made sure his old college 'buddy' pulled out and made his way down the street. When he turned around he noticed Kiara was looking too. She didn't notice him watch her as she stepped away from the window and disappear into the house. She had a sad, pained look on her face. Thomas had wounded her deeply with his comments. And Adam hated him for it.

Opening the door he could hear the soft strains of piano music, a sad composition he had never heard before. It broke his heart, because he knew Kiara well enough that she only played on two occasions. She was either very happy, or she was in pain. And it was clear to him by the sound which greeted his ears which one she was at the moment. He had to go to her and make things right before he did anything else.

***

She was beautiful in the twilight, her eyes closed with her fingers dancing over the piano keys. Her face was sad, porcelain in nature. Adam leaned against the door jam and filled the frame. Still, Kiara did not acknowledge his presence.

She continued to play. It seduced him. Her music always seduced him.

"I'm sorry about Thomas. He can be a real asshole."

"Don't worry about it. It's not like nobody knows that I'm packing on a few more pounds than the typical Adam Paul Matthews conquest is it?"

"You're not a conquest."

Kiara stopped playing and looked at him, pain riddling her gaze.

"You're a real nice guy. And you've done more than I could ever ask for. These last few months have been great, but you and I both know that I'm too cold a fish for you, and that I'm not hot enough for you to try and get past that. So, I'm going to get a shower, and I'm going to go to bed on the couch, with Chyna, per usual and then I'm going to go home tomorrow morning."

The pain which blind sided him took his breath away. This was their home. She was his girlfriend. He was her significant other. Fuck the story. And fuck Thomas Quentin.

"You can still do the story on me. I don't mind. Maybe it will be better."

"No."

"Excuse me?"

"You're staying. This is your home. Damn it, this is our home. You make breakfast. I make dinner. We can't keep our hands off of each other. You're smart, funny, and talented. We've hit the mother load."

"Don't make this any harder than it has to be."

She rose to her feet. He would not let her pass.

"Then tell me the real reason why you want to go back to that apartment without me."

She was afraid. Afraid her family would do to him what they had done to Crista. And that his family would do to her what Crista's family did. Shut her out.

It radiated from her. Fear. And it was in her eyes. Fear. He reached out for her.

"I love you Adam. I just can't bear the thought of you dying because of me."

This shocked him enough to allow her to push passed him and

lock the bathroom door shut behind her. He rushed up to behind her.

"What are you talking about?"

"Go away, all right?" her voice was deceptively calm to his ears, "don't worry about it. Just go away."

Yeah right, he thought as he tracked down the handmade key of a straightened out hanger. He loved her, and he wasn't about to give up without a fight.

***

The water came down on her face hot and welcomed, washing away the dirt and sweat from the hours spent outside mimicking Nick Ruiz's plays outside in the driveway. She wanted to cry, but she was too numb for that. Thomas Quentin was a painful reminder that there would always be someone out there who thought she and Adam made an odd pair. She wished she could be as brassy and brave as Justine, or even Crista when she'd been alive.

Then there was the fear. The fear of her family's potential damage to her life. To Adam's life. She wondered if he really knew what he was getting himself into.

But he was so wonderful. Such a waking dream come true. The

way he'd defended her honor with that ass Thomas from SI. He'd risked his dream all for her safety. And they'd shared many a steamy night. A lot of heavy petting. A lot of that. And kissing. Oh God, the kissing was enough to curl her toes. Enough to make her want to make love, to have sex, to make her forget all the shit her family had marked her with as of late. But even though she was aggressive in the sense of personality, and vigilant in the sense of protecting herself, she wanted to be seduced. She wanted him to prove to her this wasn't just a fluke, that he wasn't just using her for his own reasons. Her self-esteem wasn't in total tatters, but it was in great need of reconstruction, and getting a little help would be nice. The numbness began to ebb away, dejection starting to take it's place.

Pouring some shampoo into the palm of her hand she began to lather it through her hair. A pair of hands, not her own, wrapped around her fingers and began to wash her wet, silky, tresses. She jumped.

"Careful, or we'll both land on our asses," Adam's lips were next to her ear and his breath sent a shiver down her spine. It must've sent a shiver down her body as well because he pressed his body close to hers, before whispering huskily, "are you cold, baby?"

"No."

"Then lean your head back so I can rinse the shampoo out of your hair."

Her breath hitched, because when she tilted her head back she felt his large cock press into her back, she jerked at the sensation.

"I'm not going to hurt you. I can't wait anymore. And by the sound of it, neither can you."

His long fingers ran through her hair easily, soothing her and electrifying her at the same time. And when he snaked one arm around her chest, cupping her breast, coaxing it into a series hard peaks and a rock hard bud, she felt her knees go weak and a moan involuntarily escape her lips.

He had been waiting to feel her naked form against his for what seemed like an eternity. And her threat to leave had been a serious one, and he had to find a way to convince her to stay and this was the only way he could think of to do that.

Her skin was smooth against his coarse one, and the was she

breathed, shallow and uneven gave him hope that she would allow him to finish the seduction he'd planned for her. He kissed at her neck and moved his hand to her other breast, giving it the same time and attention he's given her other one.

"Do you like this?" he asked nipping at her ear.

"Very much so."

"Then what about this?"

Trailing his fingertips down her stomach and past her waist he parted her legs and began to stroke her sex, in soft teasing waves as he pressed his hips to her back. She gasped and groaned. His touch was expert and deft, leaving her in a heightened state of arousal.

"Yes. Oh God yes."

Her words turned him on and freed him further to play her body like the fine instrument that it was. He pressed harder onto her flesh and began to rotate his thumb in tight little circles and she began to gyrate her hips deliciously into his cock, making him so hard it hurt.

She moaned a long, gutteral, moan as he continued the assault on her sex and slid two fingers inside her. She was so hot, so tight, and so wet he thought he might lose control before either of them could fully enjoy himself. He plunged his fingers in and out of her, abandoning any sense gentility, he wanted her to feel what real passion could be about before the main course.

"Say my name, baby," he said, goading her, coaxing her, and demanding her to submit herself to him in a way only he could ask of her.

"Only if you say mine first."

This surprised him, and he realized she was seducing him as much as he was seducing her. He whispered in her ear.

"Kiara."

She began to move wildly in his arms.

"Say it again."

"Only if you say my name first."

"Adam."

She felt the climax come down on her like a thousand stars, a wave of pleasure she had never had coaxed out of her before, and as she came again and again his name rang in her mind and fell from her lips until she fell at ease in his arms and he whispered in her ear again saying, "Kiara, my sweet, sweet,

Kiara. I love you. And now I'm going to show you how much I do."
He turned her around and pushed her against the wall.

"Do you trust me?"

His eyes shone with heat, and passion, and love. And it
wiped away any of the fear she had been feeling, and washed out
the pain of Thomas Quentin and his idiocy. It didn't take long
for her to respond.

"Yes, I trust you."

"Then put me inside of you," he said lifting her leg around
his waist.

He was big, long and thick, and he jutted out to her. Just
the sight of this was beautiful as it was nestled in black curls
and would fill her up and if prowess and skill in the art of
seduction was any indication this would be a ride she would
enjoy.

She wrapped her hand around his cock and he groaned and his
body shook. She smiled as she spread her legs to allow him access
inside her. As she guided him in he surprised her by picking her
legs up and wrapping them around his waist. He thrust himself
inside her and she reveled in the feeling of being branded as

his.

He propped her up against the wall and said, "Hold on to me. Hold on tight. I'm going to erase any doubt you have about how beautiful I think you are."

He covered her mouth with his and savagely kissed her, tangling his tongue with hers and leaving no part of her mouth unexplored. With each thrust of his cock into her, he bit down on her neck, and then her ear, and then her lower lip. Their moan and groan and gasps sent him out of his mind as he lost control and thrust with an unforgiving pace into her over and over again.

Kiara had never felt so free to experience passion, and when he took her breast into his mouth she felt a much deeper, a much more intense climax starting. He suckled at her breast without mercy, biting down, laving her bruised skin, nipping at her nipple, stroking her relentlessly as he took her free breast in his mouth and started the assault on that breast. When he cupped her bottom she came and she came hard. Her body quivered, and shook, and trembled as she threw her head back and yelled out her pleasure. It seemed to go on forever, and as it ended she brought her head back down her eyes meeting a fiery, possessive gaze of her boyfriend, *her* boyfriend. He held her down on his shaft, pulled out, held her down. Pulled out, then held her down and let out a strong groan.

He lurched forward and stood their for a moment before setting her down on her feet. He pulled back and kissed her gently on her feet.

"This is your home, Kiara. In every way. Tonight, you sleep in my bed. After jury selection tomorrow we give notice on your apartment and start moving you out of it. You belong here, with me. Understand? You're beautiful, you're sensual, you everything I want in a woman. I can handle whatever you throw at me. But don't ever, ever think because of what other people ink I'm going to change my mind about you. You got all that," he said caressing her cheek.

She smiled, "I understand. As long as you understand that putting people like your old friend in their place is a pre-requisite for me staying here."

Holding Kiara close, Adam kissed her softly.

"Come on. Let's go order in."

Chapter Eleven

    Kiara looked at herself in the mirror and took several deep breaths. She hadn't fixed breakfast. She'd been avoiding Adam all morning. Her simple black suit with a creme colored blouse beneath it made her professional enough. Her hair was pulled back in a braid and her make up was minimal. She looked at least a good ten years younger than what she was. But her memories were cast in stone. And they burned bight in her mind. For herself, for Crista. She wanted Adam to understand how toxic a

relationship of any kind could be with her. But in six months
he'd held fast, casting his kindness and passion in the stone
right alongside those horrible memories. As much as she had cared
for and loved Crista, their friendship had wilted under the
fierce lights of her past. As it had reached up and snatched her
friend away from her and forced into lonely isolation until an
angry confrontation had brought her a newfound light to draw her
out of the darkness. But as she stood before the mirror, she
wondered if she would make it the duration of the trial.

Junior would have the family on his side. All of them. All
twenty-six, drug-addled, angry, members of them. The small
children, who no doubt were now living the hell she had lived
would be kept away from the proceedings, yet, they would hold her
up as what you faced if you left the fold. She shuddered. And she
mourned. She knew that for any of those little ones to have hope
she had to stand up to Junior, and pray that those twelve jurors
believed her.

A knot formed in her stomach. She moved as fast as she could
and threw up into the toilet. She tried to do this quietly, but
she was always loud when she puked. The sound of Adam walking

towards the bathroom door was in her ears, she'd left the door unlocked. Maybe because, even in all her attempts to face this alone, she wanted someone to be there. The door clicked and he was holding her hair back. She continued to vomit. He started to rub her back. Familiar territory.

What he would do to get his hands on any of them. They had tortured a child and left her to fend for herself when she needed them most. And Junior. If he ever got his hands on that bastard...he didn't want to disturb himself or Kiara with what he would do, so he took a deep breath and listened for when she was gasping for air and trying to get herself under control. Soon enough she was. And she was trying not to cry.

"I'm sorry I bothered you. I can take it from here."

She popped up and turned the sink on, and rinsed out her mouth. She began to brush her teeth. He blocked the door frame.

"You're not bothering me. You shutting me out, that's bothering me."

She scrubbed then spit out, then scrubbed and spit out again.

"You don't understand, my family is the personification of

evil. They kill everything I touch. They punish me every time they can. I don't want to expose you to that."

"The day you dropped wine on my shoes was the day you exposed me to that. How many times do I have to tell you they haven't come up against the likes of me or my family."

Washing her mouth out she searched his face for an sign of deception or weakness. Finding none she caved.

"Your sitting next to me, right?"

"Where else would I sit?"

He touched her cheek.

"Storybook. I'm your knight today. He starts giving you any trouble you look at me."

"I've been instructed to look at the prosecutor."

"Well, then pretend he's me."

A bleary smile washed its way through her eyes as she stood up on her tip toes and kissed him.

"I always pretend it's you. Just make sure you're there when I'm finished."

***

The testimony for the prosecution was winding down. It had

been two weeks of evidence, and jail house informants, and opening statements. It was coming time for her to take the stand. Everyone knew she was the lynchpin for A.D.'s case. She'd survived massive media coverage outside the courthouse. The flashbulbs, the camera lights, the microphones being thrust in her face. And through it all, Adam had guided her with care and aplomb. Showing her how to manipulate the press to her advantage and make Junior look like the slime that he was without damaging the prosecution's case.

As she and Adam walked out of the A.D.'s office they looked out in the lobby outside the courtroom she received the shock of her life. It was Michael and Helen.

"Mom? Dad?"

Kiara held her breath, what she needed now was not another round of pacifier with Adam's parents. She knew Adam loved her. But the last few months had been rocky at best with Michael and Helen. What were they doing here now?

"Son. Kiara," Michael started, but Helen cut him off.

"What your father is trying to say, is that we've watching the case on closed circuit television with the media. Vultures.

And we think we've been awful about the whole thing. Our son loves you. And he's seen fit to make that very clear by sitting at your side during this trial. It's hard for us to see that your family is throwing their weight behind the man who put you in a hospital and quite likely took the life of your friend. If you would allow it, we would like to sit with you today and for the rest of the trial."

Kiara exhaled. What had touched this woman so that it made her want to support her. Adam looked down at her.

"It's up to you. You're the one they've been hurting."

She smiled at him, then at them.

"Please, sit with us. Just leave a spot for me to sit next to Adam, okay?"

Helen held her arms open, "Come, I'm sorry I've been such a bitch. After hearing what I've heard you need us as much as you need him."

For the first time in her life Kiara felt the warmth of a mother's embrace. She was being welcomed into the fold. And it felt good. Someone cleared their throat.

"I'm sorry to interrupt, but they're calling us into the

courtroom."

Adam gave her Kiara a quick hug, "Just remember, I love you. You'll do great." He gave her gentle kiss then headed inside with his parents.

"You ready?"

"As ready as I'm going to be."

"Remember, look at me, the only time I want you to look at the defendant is when I ask you to identify him."

"Okay."

"Now, let's go get this fucker."

***

The walk to the witness stand was intimidating. To her left was her blood. People who had damaged her beyond belief. People who had taken from her time and time again and made her the villain for it. Well, not this time. This time she was going to stand up to them. If not for herself then for Crista. Crista had been dying, but they robbed her of her dignity. Robbed her of her own dignity. This time she was taking it back. She was going to put that monster where he belonged. Behind bars, with men who would make him their bitch for as long as possible.

To her right were the people who were making themselves a part of her life because they wanted to. Adam, Michael, Helen. Even Justine and Lynn were there. Over the last six months they had lifted her up, made her believe that there was hope. Something she'd grown up with very little of, something she thought there was nothing left of when she'd come home and found Crista stabbed to death in their home a year and a half ago. The cops hadn't been able to link him definitively to the case. They thought he'd done it, and they had a lot of circumstantial evidence to prove that Junior thought that Crista was her, and when he realized she wasn't he went berserk. This and so many other things raced through her mind as she was sworn in and sat down, that she didn't know if she would be able to do it. She thought of Crista, and she thought of herself, and she focused. This had to be stopped, and she was, at this time the only one who could stop him. So stop him she would.

"Would you please state your name, age, and occupation for court please."

"My name is Kiara Jackson, I'm thirty-one, and I'm currently on disability."

"Why don't you tell 'em what for you crazy bitch!" Junior shouted, standing up.

Judge Wilson, pounded her gavel and pointed at Junior, "Counsel, I suggest you tell your client to refrain himself or I'll have him removed from the court."

Junior sat back down, but not before fixing her with an intimidating glare. Kiara took a deep breath and turned back to the prosecutor. On the outside she tried to remain composed, but inside she was shaken. She wanted to look to Adam, but she had to do this on her own. She had to put this mess behind her.

"Miss Jackson, for the court's edification, what are you on disability for."

"I take it for my bi-polar disorder."

"Thank you. Now, could you please identify the man who raped you in this courtroom."

"Yes," she said, and in one powerful moment she pointed to the man who had made her life hell for the first 31 years of her life. Junior Jackson.

"Please note that the witness identified the defendant Lesley Junior Jackson. Please recount the events of March

2,2007."

"It was raining. Kind of misting. And I was feeling depressed about everything. Especially missing Crista."

An image of her holding Crispa's blood soaked body in her arms flashed in her mind. She dipped her head.

"Especially Crispa, so I went up to the Oakdale Cemetery to visit her site. I'd been there a little while when I saw Junior."

She closed her eyes and she was back there. Back at the cemetery watching Junior approach her. She tried to beat him back to her car, but he cut her off at the pass. At first he played nice.

We miss you. Please, come home.

And she'd responded, *like hell.*

Why are you doing this to us? We're blood. We're family.

And she'd said, *you murdered my friend. I'm never going anywhere with you.*

Then I guess I'll have to teach you a lesson.

He landed the first blow to her stomach, knocking her off her feet. But she'd gotten back up fast and landed a few of her own blows before the fight had gotten ruthless.

Even as she spoke on the witness stand the fight unspooled in her mind like a movie, each fly kick, every punch, each scratch for survival felt again and again as she managed to keep her eyes on the prosecutor. Before he knocked her to her back and suffocated her as he raped her. He'd left her for dead. And until she'd awakened in the hospital with Adam gazing down at her, she'd thought she was dead too.

Soon it was over. The prosecutor's questions. The memories, all of it. She had to brace herself for the defense. She only had to face one real question from him, however. And it was this.

"It was cloudy. It was raining. And everything happened so fast, can you be absolutely sure that this was the man who raped you."

"Yes."

"Positive. A lot of men fit his description."

"Yes, I'm sure."

He was trying to rattle her, but she was determined not to let him.

"You were left for dead. Do you really think your uncle would do that?"

"Yes."

"One last thing, you're estranged from your family, why is that?"

Leaning into her microphone, she fixed him with a determined stare, "It's how I'm sure he's the one who did this."

"No further questions, your Honor."

The attorney walked back to his table, flustered, angry, and upset. Judge Wilson asked, "Does the prosecution have any other witnesses?"

"No your, Honor, the prosecution rests."

"Then the witness is dismissed."

Kiara stepped down and walked to her spot next to Adam. When he squeezed her hand she was a hundred pounds lighter than she'd been in a long time. That bastard was going to pay. She hoped her testimony had everything to do with it.

***

The defense's testimony had been a cakewalk. Their tactic was to make her look like a slut. And even though it was painful, it wasn't true. The only person they could find that would testify to that was her mother and it had been fairly easy for the prosecution to minimize any type of damage that it might have done to the case. Still, one could never tell how a jury would take a rape case, even in the face of overwhelming physical evidence. Oakdale, Kentucky was no different than any other place in America in that respect. No it hadn't been the defense's case that was difficult that was hard. It was the waiting. And the longer they waited, the more Kiara feared that Junior would walk.

Her patchwork family sat in the Colonnade cafeteria, eating, waiting for word that the jury had come back. But, Kiara ate very little, drank even less and was pale as a sheet.

Everyone around her talked, but she said nothing. The possibility that Junior could walk was an outcome she'd pushed from her mind while up on the stand. Now that she waited for the verdict it was enough to make her sick all over again.

"Are you okay, Ki?" Justine asked.

"Yeah, yeah, I'm okay."

"You know you were way stronger up on the stand than I could ever be. Horatio was a pig and a violent pig, but I don't think he'd ever do what your uncle did."

"Not many people would. But I'd watch your back just the

same," Kiara said, managing a bite of the salisbury steak in front of her.

"That's what Lynn is for."

Justine smiled and kissed her girlfriend on the cheek. Lynn blushed and looked down. Justine was the more extroverted of the two. But when Lynn gazed up at Justine you could see just how deep the love went for her. The break-up must've been precipitated by Justine for some reason. Maybe she, Kiara thought, and herself should thank that pig, Horatio, she landing them in fate's path. Maybe not, as she waited for the verdict she found the knot in her stomach growing harder and harder.

"I can't eat anymore of this. I'm going to the bathroom."

Adam went to get to his feet, Kiara placed a hand on his shoulder.

"I don't need you to hold my hand, I'm a big girl. I can handle this one on my own."

With that she disappeared into the restroom.

"Mom? Justine?"

"Of course, honey."

"Sure, Adam."

The two of them followed her. About that time Adam's phone began to ring. He answered it.

"Yes. Okay, we'll be right there. Lynn, could you go fetch our girlfriends and my mother. The verdict is in."

* * *

Her heart had never hammered so hard in her life. Kiara thought she might hyperventilate. Her face was still white, but there was a little color in her cheeks, not much, but a little. And she was squeezing Adam's hand so tight that he had to squeeze back.

 He leaned down and said, "You nailed him with your testimony, just remember that. That no matter where he goes, no matter what he says, no matter what this jury says, he's already been convicted by your courage to stand up to his evil. Okay?"

She looked up at him and tried to smile and nod.

"It's going to be all right."

It was the voice of Helen, she smiled supportively the then laid her arm across her shoulders.

"Your courage will be rewarded."

Kiara hoped they were right. That Junior would pay. The

monster had never paid in the past. He always found a way to wriggle free from the law, a way to cut her off from the few family members who had supported her the first go around. She had thrown up in the bathroom at the Colonnade. She hoped she did not do it again.

"Bailiff, would you please show the jury in."

The seven men and five women walked in. Each of them looking only at the judge. They had taken four hours to deliberate her life and Junior's future. She tried to keep the knot down in her belly as the seconds passed.

"On the charge of Rape in the First Degree what say you?"

"In the case of the State of Kentucky versus the defendant, Lesley 'Junior' Jackson, guilty, of Rape in the First Degree."

A wave of relief began to encompass Kiara as the knot in her stomach dissolved and she fell against Adam and she began to sob softly. Adam wrapped her up tight and began to stroke her hair, kissing the top of her head.

"And on the charges of Attempted Murder what say you?"

"We the jury, in the case of the State of Kentucky versus the defendant, Lesley 'Junior' Jackson, find the defendant guilty, of Attempted Murder."

The courtroom on Junior's side erupted in outrage and the judge struggled to maintain order. But to Kiara it was all a blur. Her demon was to be put behind bars. Her knight was holding fast to her. And a new network was at her call. Life was starting over, and it was hers to do with what she pleased.

***

"Here."

Adam strode over to the couch and set a huge bowl of popcorn down in Kiara's lap before curling up with her on the couch. He kissed her on the cheek.

"I'm proud of you, baby."

She blessed him with a tired smile and leaned against him.

"I'm just glad the bastard is behind bars."

"The way he's hurt you, the way they've hurt you. I wish I could make it all go away."

"Maybe one day it won't matter anymore, and they'll just leave me alone."

"I'll make sure of it."

She laughed softly.

"Are you my knight?"

"Yes, I most certainly am."

"Too bad you weren't when I was younger."

"Too bad nobody was."

"Yeah, but I survived didn't I?"

"Yeah, I guess you did."

He gazed into her eyes and remembered the fragile woman in the hospital bed. The one who had opened her eyes and made him love her. Right then, right there. She smiled.

"What?"

"Kiara."

"Yes."

"Will you marry me?"

She blinked. Her heart skipped a beat. Had she heard him correctly?

"Well? Will you?"

Forgetting the popcorn she threw her arms around his neck and began to cry, she looked up at him.

"Please tell me you're not teasing me. I couldn't take it after the last month I've had."

Pushing the hair back from her face he kissed her with tenderness and sweetness.

"I would never tease or lie to you about something like this. Will you marry me, and take my name?"

She kissed him with such passion it almost made him forget what he asked.

"Yes, Adam. If you mean it yes I'll marry you. Yes I'll take your name. I just hope your parents can handle it."

"They like you Kiara, better than that, they respect you. And yes, I mean it."

Chyna leapt up onto the couch and meowed. Adam pet her and she purred.

"Yes, you little furball I mean it. And that means you can stay," he said with a playful grin.

Pushing him to his back, Kiara crawled on top of him and whispered.

"Yes, Adam Paul Matthews, I'll marry you. And I'll love you forever for asking me."

"No, your saying yes will make me forever love you."

He kissed her, and he felt what eternity could be in that

kiss. He kissed her again, and again, and again. He would love her forever. Until the day he died.

Chapter Twelve

Nick Ruiz turned to his assistant Camron Ori and grimaced. The team was not coming along as quickly as he would like. He'd been hired to make big things happen at UK, and if he didn't produce he would be out on his ass for sure. With pressure coming from the fans and his wife he wondered why he had taken this job. Then he saw what his assistant was staring at.

Jason Dexter.

The boy stole the ball ran the length of the floor and

dished a no look pass to a fellow teammate. It had been textbook perfect. But he had a rule. And everyone had to adhere to it. Even the most talented ones who gave them hope. Even the ones who reminded him of the reason he'd taken the job to begin with.

"Dexter."

He shot the ball again before coming over. This, infuriated Nick. When he called he expected the player to come, not fuck around.

"Dexter!"

The young man trotted over with a self satisfied grin on his face. If it was possible to be angrier with the kid he had just done it.

"What did I tell you to do?"

"To come over here."

"Then why didn't you?"

"I had the ball in my hands," the kid was smirking now.

"I don't know how things worked on your last team, kid, but you're a freshman on the Wildcats now and there will be no showboating and there will be no shot taken unless I call it. Even in practice. You do it and you will either do laps or the team will do suicides, my choice, understand?"

"I don't play for you, I play for Kentucky."

"I don't care who you are. Steps. Until I say stop. Because, understand kid, as long as you play for Kentucky, you play for me. I own you until graduation day. And unlike past coaches, if you don't go pro early, your ass will graduate. Now, steps."

Jason Dexter was a junior on the team. Who, up until that point, been the defacto leader. The past few years had been tumultuous. Nick understood that. He understood that Tubby had had the shitty task of following in Rick Pitino's shoes. No one would ever be Pitino to the Big Blue Nation. Not even him. So that wasn't his deal. He wasn't even going to try. But these boys were like the inmates running the asylum. That was going to change. And having the most talented, the most head strong, the most arrogant and unruly member of the team who was defying him at every turn, run the steps at Rupp Arena was the first step to breaking these boys down and building them back up.

At first the kids kept running their drills with the coaches. But eventually they saw Dexter running the steps, and that he, their coach, was refusing to let up on their leader.

They started to stare. It was having it's preferred effect.

"See that boys? Because, that's what you are, you're kids, you're not men. Not yet. But, if you stick with me, by the end of it, you will be. But, there will be no defiance. There will be no showboating, and there will be no rule breaking. If there is, you face anything from running steps, to being benched for as long as I see fit. And I don't care when the infraction is committed, punishment will be enforced as I see fit. Now get back to practice. What I'm doing right now is of no concern to you."

Dexter was fading pretty badly. He'd been running steps for twenty minutes. Almost twenty-five. It would take more than this to break Dexter down, but this was a good start. It was time to ease up on the kid. For now.

"Hey, Dexter. That's enough, come over here."

The boy walked over. Sweat pouring off of him. Hands on his hips. Gasping for air. When he got over to Nick he leaned over, trying not to retch.

"Do you understand why you ran for so long?"

"No I don't coach."

"That's a shame. I pictured you as a leader. I guess I was

wrong."

"But I am a leader. This is my team."

"Funny, I thought this was Kentucky's team."

"This is Big Blue Nation's team. And as long as I play for them, I play for you."

Nick smiled. At least the kid wasn't stupid.

"Coach, you're smiling, does that mean I can?"

Nick laughed inside, he would have to share that one with Camron.

"No, it doesn't. But you can go back to practicing."

"Coach?"

"Yes, Dexter."

"Could I get some Powerade?"

"Make it fast."

His player trotted off. More like shuffled off. Nick could see where the kid's leg muscles could very easily cramp up. Maybe he had forced him to run to much. Nick shook the thought off as quickly as it had settled. He refused to go soft. He had a program to rebuild. It was what the fans demanded of him. It was what his athletic director demanded of him. It was what he demanded of himself.

***

Nick felt good as he walked into his and Rhiannon's new home. It was six thousand square feet of heaven. A perfect place for he and his wife to grow a family in. But it was quiet. And the unmistakable aroma of take out was missing. He knew he was late. But it was only fifteen minutes and for him that was a new world record. He was always late, and he was trying real hard to please her. Removing his coat he felt something vibrating in his pocket, it was his cell phone, and it was his wife on the other end. He answered it.

"Rhiannon."

"Don't you fucking Rhiannon me. I've been trying to get a hold of you for the last hour," she sounded angry, but there was something else in her voice, fear.

"Calm down, honey, I'm sorry, I didn't hear the phone. I would've of answered you if I had."

That seemed to quell the anger, but when she spoke again her voice was filled with tears and anguish.

"My water broke, they're going to have to take the baby."

"Where are you?"

"Oakdale Hospital. Room 222."

"I'll be there in ten minutes."

"Nick, I'm sorry."

"Don't worry about being sorry. I'm here to take all the abuse you can dish out."

"It's not that..."

The sound of her sucking air through clenched teeth came through the receiver.

"Don't sweat the small stuff. And it's all small stuff right now. Just concentrate on holding that baby in until I get there. I love you."

"Just hurry, okay?" she was weeping now.

"Okay, I'm on my way."

He closed his cell and tucked it away. As he raced out the door he had an odd feeling the pit of his stomach. Something in the way Rhiannon had sounded. A fear fell over him. Not just about the baby, but over Rhiannon as well.

***

Adam and Kiara walked through the Highlands of Oakdale.

Poking through every shop, listening to records at Ear-Xtacy, and enjoying a poetry reading and coffee at the Twice Told Café. Adam leaned forward, gazing at her as if she were the only one in the room.

"There is a piano up on that stage. Why don't you go play that new piece you've been working on?"

"Why don't you do it?" she laughed.

"You're good, Kiara. Really, really good. You deserve to be heard."

"What do you know about how good I am, you're my fiancé. You're supposed to think I'm good."

"Listen, I wouldn't let you go up there if I thought you couldn't handle it."

The coffee shop was small in nature, allowing for an intimate setting and sound. Deep down she knew that Adam was on to something with her and her steps into the world of concert piano. She doubted the high class world of composers would ever allow her in to do as she pleased. But Adam told her that didn't matter. That doing the one thing that you loved was the only thing that mattered. She had taught Crispa that lesson, and she

had been on the verge of success when Junior had changed all
that.

"Kiara?"

She shook her head.

"I'm fine."

"Then play the piano."

"I've never played in public before."

"Before you I'd never fell so hard so fast. It's your turn
to walk the tightrope."

"Oh alright. I'll do it. But if I suck it's your fault."

She smiled, but something about her was different, she
glowed, and her eyes shone when she looked at him before walking
up to the piano and sitting down at it. He watched her flex her
fingers and take a few deep breaths before she launched into a
melancholic melody. And she was beautiful. So beautiful. A little
different from the girls who had caught his eye in the past, but
she had fly-kicked her way into his heart and from that moment on
he hadn't let go. She deserved the world and he planned on giving
it to her.

The music enveloped her, haunted her, and told the story of

her life. She smiled as the melody carried her further and further away from the coffee shop and into the future with Adam and their family. She smiled again, she hadn't told Adam, but they would have to move the wedding date up if she were to fit into a wedding gown. At least one that she wanted. So on and on she played, not noticing the crowd she had drawn until she stopped. A rousing applause broke her from her train of thought and she blushed. Adam stuck his fingers in his mouth and gave a loud whistle. She blushed again and quickly left the stage.

"I am so going to kick your ass when we get home."

A wicked grin crossed his lips, "Promise?"

She punched him in the arm.

"Let's go before it gets too dark to walk home, besides I need to tell you something and I don't want an audience for it."

"Oh come on, tell me now."

"No."

"What if I promise you special favors later on tonight."

"That's what got us into this mess in the first place."

His eyes lit up and they rushed out the door and he lifted her up off her feet and twirled her around before setting her back down on the ground.

"Are you serious? A baby?"

"I had it confirmed today at the doctor's office. Two months."

He twirled her around again, kissing her this time.

"You have the ability to make a rough around the edges, big girl like me feel like I can have the storybook."

"You've given me the one thing I can't do without."

"A baby?"

"No. You."

Taking her hand in his they walked along in silence for a while.

"I can't wait to tell Mom and Dad. They've always wanted grandchildren. Now I can give them one."

"If it's a boy what would you name him?"

"Lucas. Lucas Matthews has a nice ring to it. What about a girl, what would you name her?"

"Crispa Matthews."

He squeezed Kiara close and kissed her at her temple.

"I love you, Kiara Jackson."

She gazed up at him.

"I love you too, Adam Paul Matthews."

Something up ahead caught Adam's attention. A car with someone hanging the window, the sound of pop-pop-popping up and down the street.

"Get behind me."

"What?"

"Get behind me!"

He shoved her behind him and down to the ground and jerked one-two-three times before crumpling to the ground on top of her. The spraying of bullets continued up and down the street. Kiara wriggled up from beneath him and saw the damage. Blood poured from his stomach and chest. She touched and began to shake. Not again. Not again. Not again.

She looked to his face, a trickle of blood was coming from his mouth.

"Don't you dare die on me. I need you. We need you. You got that?"

He reached up and touched her face.

"You can do this," his voice was raw and ragged.

"I can't lose you."

Someone had walked up and stooped down with a cell phone.

"What street are we on honey?"

"Highland Avenue."

The man looked away. It was not his moment to share.

Kiara held Adam's hand to her face.

"Don't go. Don't go."

Adam struggled to breathe as he looked into Kiara's eyes. He didn't want to go. But he was growing cold. The man with the cell phone took off his suit jacket and pressed down on his wounds. Adam touched her stomach.

"You've got to take care of her."

Through tears she asked, "How do you know it's a her?"

His eyes closed and he said, "Because she told me."

His breathing shallowed, struggled, then stopped altogether. A fire of the deepest pain imaginable ripped through her soul as she sobbed and sobbed and sobbed.

Nick could hear the sirens coming. His heart broke for her, as he looked at down at the man who had given his life to protect his wife, or his fiancé, whatever, and their unborn child. What he would do for a love like that. What he would do for a wife like that. What he would do to be a man like that.

As the ambulance pulled up to take them away he told the paramedics to take them to Oakdale Hospital. And that when the bill came just to forward it to him, Nick Ruiz. What he would do to be a man like that.

***

Nick came bursting through the delivery room door with his surgical gown on to see a pale and sweaty Rhiannon. She did not smile when she saw him. And there was another man in the delivery room who was not the doctor. It was a junior partner from Fredrick, Martin, and Straus. William something or another.

"I waited for you, I called you, and still you didn't come. I had to call William."

"You had to call a man who lives down in Florida to come be in our delivery room? I don't understand."

Rhiannon looked away. The baby was wheeled in. She had arrived safely and without problems.

"Now isn't the time to discuss this Nick," William said gazing down at the baby, "she has your eyes Rhiannon."

Rhiannon looked up at William, "Do you want to hold her?"

"Excuse me, don't you think the father should get to hold the baby first?"

He was trying to remain calm as the dread which had fallen over him in his kitchen came over him again. Only this time it was followed by the hot stab of anger. William looked up.

"Now don't do anything stupid, Nick. There's a child to consider. And you haven't been checked into your marriage for a very long time."

Nick was shocked that a virtual stranger would talk to him in such a way. But even though William was a stranger to him it was clear he was anything but to his wife.

"I'm sorry Nick, you said ten minutes and suddenly it was an hour. I couldn't wait any longer."

"It couldn't be helped, Rhiannon."

She sighed, "It never can be with you and those boys can it?"

"If you must know a man was murdered protecting his fiancé and unborn child. I had a cell phone and helped them out best I could."

"I was having a baby."

Keeping a lid on his anger best he could Nick he gazed at the lost opportunity.

"You know, I watched that man die. I watched him use his dying words to comfort a woman who loved him deeply. It was awful to watch them being torn apart. Now I don't feel so bad in asking for a divorce."

"What?"

"You let William hold that child first. It's obvious who you think the father of the child is."

"That doesn't mean I don't love you."

"The sad thing is, that doesn't mean I don't love you either."

"So what does this mean."

"It means you can go back to Florida and live the happy life for yourself that you've been imagining for the last six months."

"Nick..."

She called after him, but the pain and anguish was too great to turn around. Between his obsession with his team and her infidelity he knew they would never be able to make things work.

Not here. Not in Kentucky. Not where college basketball was life, and if he could win he'd be something of a god to the fans. And he loved college basketball. The next woman in his life would have to have a better understanding of that. Someone who loved the sport like he did. And whose whole life revolved around the sport. He didn't know if a woman like that existed. But he hoped that she did. Because he needed to replace the angry, bitter, taste this life choice was leaving in his mouth.

***

Kiara sat at his bedside holding Adam's hand and brushing a few stray strands of hair back from his face. Helen and Michael had already come into the room and said their goodbyes. She had been afraid Helen would blame her for the death of her son. But she had not. She understood that some things were just acts of random violence. As a mother she grieved like no other. So Kiara didn't but in when Helen and Michael went in first. She'd stood out in the hallway alone. Numb with rage and grief that if there was a God that he would do something like this again to her after everything she'd been through. But now she was at Adam's side, tears sliding down her cheeks. And scared of what the future held for her.

"Why'd you leave me? Why didn't you twist around and fall on top of me that way instead of taking the shots in the front?"

She was angry. So angry. And so grief stricken she couldn't think straight. She laid her head at his chest and cried. She cried so hard it hurt. And the more she tried not to cry, the harder she did cry. There was no one to comfort her in this moment. No one really understood what she was feeling. The loss of a man who had given her everything she could have ever wanted in life. The loss of a man who had loved her like she loved him. It was too hard to bear, she thought she might go mad with the pain she was feeling. It was all too much. Today was supposed to be a happy day. She was pregnant with his child. Their child. She had never thought she'd want to be pregnant. But now that she was it was the last piece of Adam that she had. And she would not let go of her. She believed Adam was right. They would have a girl.

She continued to cry. The pain was just too great not to.

I'm here Kiara Matthews. I will always be here for as long as you need me. Whenever you need me. Please, don't cry. I weep enough for the both of us from this side of life.

She kept her cheek at his chest and the sobbing subsided, but not the pain.

"I love you, Adam Paul Matthews. And I always will."

She sat up, kissed his lips sweetly.

"And I promise you, your daughter will know you. And know all the great things about you, and how you saved my life."

She kissed his cheek, then touched it. She realized she had to leave now, because if she didn't she would grieve herself straight down into the grave with him in less than the time it had taken him to die in her arms. She stood, took a breath, and prepared to tell his parents she was pregnant.

Chapter Thirteen

Nick had been sitting in the hospital chapel for a long time. The burn of his wife's infidelity and the loss of a child he thought was his was heavy on his soul. It angered him beyond measure. And yet, he had coldly cut his wife off at the knees and left her with the man who had been making her feel understood and loved and wanted. So, as angry as he was, he knew that this feeling of loss was wholly his wife's doing, that in some small measure she had not felt right in the marriage or she would not have turned outside of it. But he was a man. And he had never turned to a woman other than Rhiannon. His only mistress was basketball and she knew that when she married him. He struggled with how to carry himself. He didn't cry. Because men in his family did not cry. They did not talk about their feelings. If they were angry they fought. Yelled and screamed if it was a woman. Fought it out if it was a man. And he had tried not to do that with Rhiannon. But old tapes died hard and he was sure he'd done enough to at least drive a wedge between them. He wondered, had she loved him, or had she married him to please her family? He guessed he would never know. In some ways he didn't want to know. And a bitter part of him wanted to leave her with nothing.

The sounds of shuffling feet jerked him out of his downward spiral as he turned his head to the side to see who had joined him. The choked sobs were wrenching to hear and he decided to leave whoever it was alone and go home. He was sitting in the back so when the woman passed him he could see who she was. She was the woman he'd stopped on the street for before coming to his wife. The woman didn't notice him. She walked up to the front of the chapel and spit at the crucifix. She leaned forward opened her mouth and let out the loudest mournful, angriest, wordless cry he'd ever heard. It startled him and punched him in the gut. He looked over his shoulder as the cry lasted for several seconds, before dropping off and turning into reckless sobs. She leaned forward again, opened her mouth and began to scream again. Nick quickly shut the door to the chapel as her cry reverberated in his ears.

"Why'd you take him from me! Why God damn it! Why!"

She spit at the crucifix again, only this time she looked ready to scale the wall so that she could tear it down. Nick made a decision. A split second decision, one he would never be able to explain, but one he would never regret. He ran up the small aisle and pulled her back. This earned him an elbow to the stomach, a stomped foot, and a crack to the jaw, which had he not pulled away when he did would have been have been more painful than it was.

"Whoa, whoa, whoa," he said holding her wrists together.

She was grief stricken, but there was something else in those eyes, rage. A rage that could overpower the strongest of men. Including him, so he let go. She may have been a big girl, but she, with that look, and that grief for the man she loved, had taken his breath away. He thought of Rhiannon holding the baby, and for a second he felt the pain of loss. But it did not compare to what he was witnessing right then. She still loved the man who had given his life for her. And she was not dealing with it well at all.

"I'm not here to hurt you or scare you. I'm just here to help you. Is there someone I can get or call for you?"

She shook her head no. "I just want to be left alone."

"I can't do that. I have to make sure you're okay."

"I'm fine. Isn't your wife having a baby or something?"

"How'd you know that?"

"It's all over the news these days. When you're the head coach of the University of Kentucky Wildcats men's basketball team you tend to live your life under a microscope. Go to her. I'm a fan, she's your wife."

He put an arm around her and led her to a pew. After they sat down he said, "She won't be for much longer. But I think you need someone right now more than I do."

"Come on. Who am I? I'm a nobody. A pregnant nobody. Who is

still wearing her engagement ring," he bit her bottom lip, "what the fuck am I going to do?"

"You have family right?"

She doubled over and started to cry again.

"What, did I say something?"

"My family are dead to me," her words tumbled out in a rushed cadence, filled with anger and pain.

"What about his family?"

She cried. They had been happy with the kind of muted joy she had feared they would have.

"They had just warmed up to me. The baby thing in the face of what has just happened is too much for the time being."

He tugged her up and reached into his pocket, drawing out a handkerchief.

"Here, you need this more than I do."

She smiled at him. Wow. Even through the tears she lit up from the inside with a kind of beauty that Rhiannon had never possessed. Even while pregnant, even as she held what he thought for so briefly was his child.

"What's your name? You know mine, so I only think it fair

that I know yours."

"Kiara Jackson. I'm stuck with a last name I hate. A name I despise. Because some piece of shit decided to spray Highland Avenue with bullets," she started to cry again.

His heart broke for her, and he leaned her against his chest.

"It's okay. Take his last name anyway. He was willing to give it to you."

"I can't afford it."

"Why not?"

"I don't want to talk about it."

"All right. We'll figure something out."

She cried so hard it soaked his shirt and her shoulders shook. Between her pain and his he felt his own heart break.

"I love him."

"I know."

"I always will."

Nick wondered how anyone could love anyone else like that. Above themselves. Above God. Above life itself.

"Mr. Ruiz."

"Yes Kiara."

"Thank you for stopping."

He wrapped her up in a tight embrace and let her cry. It wasn't so loud or so long now. But as she cried he wondered if he, in the face of this, had any right to mourn his loss at all.

* * *

A soft knock at his office door disturbed him from the basketball film he was watching of his Kentucky's first opponent, the Generals of Indiana. The light from the television reflected like a projector on his face. He looked up. It was Jason. He smiled.

"Dexter, what can I do ya' for."

"I just wanted to come by and say how sorry I am that you're going through what you are."

Nick hadn't wanted his boys to find out about his divorce and that whole mess the way that they had. It underminded his authority, they would see him as weak and ineffective. And he was just beginning to get through to some of them.

"These things happen. Even to coaches. But thank you."

"It's not every day that a stranger stops and helps someone

who's been shot. Especially from where I'm from."

"Oh," Nick couldn't hide the look of surprise on his face. He planned on going to the funeral the next day. But he'd wanted it to be kept low key, "how'd you find out about that?"

"It's been on the news since last night. I'm proud to call you coach, Coach."

Nick smiled warily, "Then does that mean you're going to listen to me during practice and not showboat during games?"

"You're funny, Coach."

"Jason, I watched a man die yesterday in the arms of a woman he was protecting. And it made me realize something."

"What's that?"

"That if it's the last thing I do I'm going to whip this team into a national championship contender."

"Coach, we play for Kentucky. We are championship contenders."

"Wrong. You've got to earn the right to wear that Wildcat jersey before you ever think about being a contender for something other than second place, in a tie no less, in the eastern division of the Southeastern Conference."

"Hey," Jason tried to protest.

"Hay's for horses, and being a Wildcat is about a whole lot more than just suiting up. It's about pride, honor, and excellence. It's about bringing your best game every night and not bitching and moaning that you don't have the ball enough. And if you don't believe that you know you can leave any time you like."

"Are you okay, Coach?"

"I'm fine. I'll see you tomorrow at practice."

"Nine-thirty, right?"

"No, one in the afternoon."

"I thought UK basketball was all about pride, and honor, and not being a ball hog."

Nick's face went stone still.

"I'm going to a funeral and a burial. I should make you go with me."

"Who's funeral? That guy you tried to help?"

Nick turned away, and continued to watch the film.

"I should make you go just to teach you a lesson. But I'm not going to make them suffer for your attitude."

"Whatever, Coach. I'll see you tomorrow."

"And we'll start with steps until I say you've had enough."

"Oh c'mon."

"You made your bed. Now you're going to have to lay in it."

Jason mumbled under his breath.

"Do you want to add suicides to that?"

"No."

"Then go before you say something else really stupid."

"Bye, Coach."

"Bye."

Jason Dexter was proving to be a tough nut to crack. He was better, but he was still a ball hog, and had yet to completely buy into his system.

But as he watched the film of the Generals running the floor he was worried. Worried that his young team had yet to conform to his way of thinking, worried that their egos surpassed their talent, and worried that he wouldn't have their leader ready in time.

★

The service was larger than expected. Lots of people she did not know. People from Adam's past. Family. College buddies. And women. Lots and lots of women. All of them crying. There was one in particular that Kiara noticed. She was petite, with honey blonde hair and sparkling blue eyes. She was an absolute knock out. Helen saw Kiara staring in the woman's direction.

"Ignore her and she'll go away," Helen whispered below the din of tears and talking.

"Who is that?"

"That's the woman who broke my son's heart. I don't understand why she's even here."

"Is that Layla?"

"Ignore her."

But it was too late. Layla was already upon them. She looked at Helen and Michael and smiled sadly.

"I'm so sorry. When I heard the news I had to come pay my respects."

"Good. Now that you've paid your respects you can go sit with the rest of them," Helen said.

"I know you're hurting, but I loved him too."

Kiara looked around the sanctuary of the Oakdale Funeral

Home and swallowed the urge to fly-kick the woman down the aisle and straight out the front door. Michael stepped in to quell the situation.

"Thank you for coming Layla, but there's only enough room for family up here."

Layla looked at Kiara.

"Adam never told me he had a sister."

"He doesn't," Helen said with a smile on her face, "this is his fiancé."

The look on her face said it all. The need to put Layla in her place was overwhelming.

"Still, I'm not like a lot of the women in this room, I had a relationship with him. I'm sure there's some room up here for me. And I'm sure..."

"Kiara. And yes. I do mind. Find somewhere else to sit."

Michael cleared his throat.

"You heard the lady. Move on Layla. You're not wanted here."

Layla gave Kiara a nasty up and down. Kiara responded in kind.

"He loved me you know."

"Yeah. And you shit on him for it. He loved me too, whether you like it or not. So why don't you leave me and them, alone for good."

Layla was taken aback and made a hasty retreat.

Helen put an arm around her and led them to the front row. There they sat and watched, and listened, and cried as people spoke about how Adam had touched their lives in some fashion or another.

Kiara cried and cried and cried until she was numb. Until she felt nothing. They seemed to be coming to an end when one last person came walking up to the podium. He moved fast, his charcoal suit jacket swinging back and forth behind him. If she had been paying attention to him she would have recognized him straight away. But she wasn't and she hadn't. Not until he turned and shook hands with one of the ministers overseeing the service. His smooth, charismatic eyes swept over the audience and her disbelief slammed into her numbed state, jarring the pain loose once again.

When he spoke his voice was silk. And in his delivery he, hands down, encapsulated the moment without the trite he was a great man triteness, or God calls home his favorites first bullshit.

"My name is Nick. I'm new around here."

A few soft laughs were offered up. Kiara smiled a bit through her tears. Adam would have liked that.

"But I'm not the one who today is about. And even though those who loved him best take comfort in God, I'm not sure He's the one who today is about. Today is about Adam. And I don't use his name as if I knew him personally as a friend. I use Adam in the sense as in the few moments I was privileged to know him. I knew Adam Paul Matthews as a man. And that, is the highest privilege of all. He died protecting those he loved most. His soon to be wife, and their unborn child. We should all hope to die with the dignity he did, comforting Kiara with his final words. Adam is the kind of man we men should all aspire to be like. And we should all hope to find the kind of love he found in the arms of Kiara. And should we all find a woman like Kiara to turn to in our time of need. Because I can tell you from the short time I have known her, no one else I have ever known, loved so deeply, so completely another human being."

Just as quickly as he came, Nick Ruiz departed and seated himself at the back of the sanctuary. Kiara felt a wave of peace wash over her. As if Adam were sitting there with her. She looked over her shoulder and caught Nick's gaze. She mouthed, 'Thank you.' He nodded his head and responded in kind, 'You're welcome.' She turned back around and wiped away a few stray tears. There would always be tears for what might have been, and part of her would mourn Adam forever. But she placed her hand on her stomach and breathed deeply, a part of Adam would always be with her. She had to remember that.

Chapter Fourteen

It had been two months since Adam had died and Helen and Michael had decided Kiara could stay in the house. It only made sense they reasoned. Adam had loved her more than he'd loved any

of the other women he'd brought around. And there had been a lot
of them. Including Layla. That bitch really pissed her off. She'd
made such a show of it one would have thought she was the
grieving fiancé. But Nick had been incredible. He'd swept in and
plucked her from the crowd and treated her for what she was. A
spurned lover. He wasn't mean. He was just firm and let it be
known who was the one with the right to be carrying on if they so
chose. Only Kiara didn't share her grief hysterically in public.
She tried to breakdown when she thought no one was looking. And
there had been many times in the last few months that she didn't
think she could take it anymore. The only thing that kept her
hanging in there was their baby. Little Crispa. That's what she
called her. It's what she insisted Justine and Lynn call the
baby. It's what she demanded of Michael and Helen.

But this was not a good night. This was hell. She sat in
front of Adam's computer and she was reading his brilliant
article called Number 1. He made her look like a survivor. A
champion. A great couch coach. A savant. He even used the word
gifted. All that was left to do was call Thomas and tell him the
article was done. There was something so final about it.

Something that said, Adam is no more, that this was his last word. On her, on their life together. She didn't want to think about it. But there it was, staring her in the face. She needed to call Thomas. She really did. But it felt like a goodbye. She touched her stomach. But she had to do this. It was one of the last things he did. She had to see it through. Flipping through Adam's rolodex he came to Sports Illustrated, with Thomas Quentin's extension printed neatly below it. Kiara picked up the phone and dialed.

"Quentin. Spill it Matthews. I've been waiting for your article for two months."

A lump formed in her throat, but she swallowed it down.

"I have the article, Thomas. Adam won't be able to give it to you."

"What are you talking about? If he doesn't get on this phone and give me a damn good reason why I should run a two month late article, the piece won't run."

"He's dead."

"Ha ha, very funny. Put the guy on the phone."

"Shut up and listen because I'm not going to say it again.

Adam isn't here anymore. He died two months ago when some guy, who they still haven't caught, shot him three times. Now I'm alone. I'm pregnant. And I'm putting his affairs in order. A little help from you would be nice."

Silence greeted her ears.

"Why didn't you call me?"

"I'm calling you now. That'll have to do."

It sounded like he was stifling some tears.

"Alright. Email it to me. I'll have a photographer down there on Friday. I'll call Nick Ruiz and see about getting you a jersey specially fitted, and getting a shot on the locker room."

"Maybe we should go a different route. His plate is kind of full right now."

"You are a fan. I hear Nick helped out a couple...you mean that was you and Adam?"

"Yes. And if you don't mind I think it best if you laid off of him."

"What, are you friends?"

"No, but any man who shows the kind of character he did in helping me and Adam deserves consideration."

"How about this, I call him, then send the article. If it's good enough."

She could feel her temper rising.

"You know it's good enough. And if it doesn't run in your fucking magazine, or I will come to your house and personally kick your ass."

"Yeah? How do you know where I live?"

"It's called a rolodex you prick. Just run it."

Kiara hung up and started to hurl the phone through the air, but she held on. Nick Ruiz would always hold a special place in her heart for many reasons. Even if he wasn't able to fix Kentucky's ails, there would be a good feeling for the man for her own reasons. He'd called her a few times. Come by just to check on her. The chats were never long, and neither were his visits. But they were always sincere, always kind. He always brought something with him. Groceries. Cat food. A check to cover Adam's burial costs. Nick was a good man, a lot like Adam was. Just more intense and ambitious. More focused too. But in the end, no one was like Adam. No one. Still, with a nasty divorce and the spotlight already blistering on his coaching abilities,

Nick Ruiz didn't deserve to bothered over an article for Sports Illustrated. Especially a piece that Thomas Quentin could claim as his own.

Not a few seconds had passed when the phone rang again. She was tired. The battle with Thomas had taken it out of her. She checked the caller i.d. A bright spot. Nick. Maybe they were friends. And God knew she needed friends. Justine and Lynn had been wonderful. And Michael and Helen were making themselves as available to her as they could. But Thomas was not her friend. The man was a leech, and she couldn't wait to be done with him.

"Hello."

"Hey there you."

He was drunk. She could hear it in his voice.

"Nick? Where are you?"

"Alone, at home, drinking a twelve year old scotch. Care to join me?"

"Why the hell would I do that?"

"Because friends don't let friends drink alone."

"I don't drink."

"Why can't you?"

"You don't know me well enough for that kind of information."

"That's a shame."

"What? That I don't drink?"

"No, that we're not better friends."

Kiara's mouth went dry. And her heart squeezed. Then she felt a stab of grief and anger. She was still grieving, Nick knew this. Why was he calling her.

"Nick, why are you really calling me. I know it's not to flirt. You know how I'm feeling these days."

"Why can't I flirt with you? You're beautiful, Kiara. You glow. When you've been playing when I've dropped by it's been magic. I think about you a lot Kiara. It's hard to keep it to myself."

"You're drunk. Sleep it off, call me in the morning if you need to talk to me."

"C'mon, I'm lonely. And I haven't made a lot of friends over the last few months."

"What about your coaches?"

"Their wives aren't keen on drunks talking to their

husbands."

"You are at home."

"I'm in bed with the bottle."

"Jesus."

"No, just Nick."

"God, alright, I'll bite. Why are you alone drinking what is probably a very expensive bottle of scotch?"

A sigh a swish of liquid poured into the silence.

"Divorce was finalized today."

"Oh. Sorry to hear that, it's not easy to lose what you did."

"No, it's not easy to lose what you did. Losing what you did is a crime. Losing what you did makes losing what I did a joke."

"Listen, Nick. You thought you were going to be a father. You thought you had it all. The wife, the home, the career, the family. It's devastating. You loved her. At least what you thought she was. I don't suggest you drink your way through it, though."

"I don't want to be alone."

"You have a nation at your feet."

"I don't call my nation to comfort me."

"I'm a part of that nation."

"No. You're my friend."

A man's qualification for what made someone their friend was funny. But Nick was a special kind of guy. His heart was bleeding. Even though she was having a hard time of it, maybe it would do her some good to help someone else right now.

"Nick."

"C'mon, come over Kiara. I know it's not good for you to sit around doing what you're doing."

"If you don't shut up I might change my mind. Let me grab a pen."

Kiara pulled a scrap of paper from the printer and fished around for an ink pen.

"Tell me how I get to your place."

"Take I-65 North to Watterson East. Then take the Breckenridge Ln exit. Turn left until you get to Lake Forest. Turn left onto Altshelter. It dead ends. My house number is 3456. It has a big blue K flag flying from it."

"If I get lost I'm hunting you down and kicking your ass."

"Funny. I here that's what you said to Thomas Quentin of Sports Illustrated."

"Christ. This isn't about that is it?"

Another swish of liquid.

"No. I need a friend. Not a publicity stunt."

"You better be telling the truth."

"May I run out of scotch and never drink a drop again."

Yeah. Right. Nick Ruiz didn't strike her as the kind of man who had gotten where he had by tipping his hand to everyone he knew. She hoped she wasn't walking into the lion's den with a piece of raw meat hanging from her neck.

***

The house was huge. Six thousand square feet easy. It looked like an old plantation style mansion. It was white with tall pillars and a wrap around deck. The oak sign hanging next to the door still read 'The Ruizs'. As blitzed as Nick was it didn't surprise Kiara the sign was still up. The warm breeze blew hard and a rumble of thunder ripped through the air. Knocking on a door of a house of this size would not do. Kiara was counting on the idea that perhaps Nick had passed out so that she could get the hell out of there. Because she was an Oakdale kind of girl in a Lake Forest kind of world, and she, in the dark of night, did not fit in. Pulling the glass door back she pressed the doorbell, then knocked. No answer. She pressed the doorbell and knocked again. Still no answer. She reached out to ring the bell again when she hesitated. What the fuck was she doing?

It was close to midnight. It had taken her forever to find the place. And she was in mourning. What on earth was she doing at a man's home. A man who had been there at a really bad time for her, but a man she didn't actually know that well. She took a deep breath and remembered the moment in the hospital chapel. And she remembered the man who sat with her as the love of her life passed away in her arms. Hard stuff. Tough stuff. Even if Rhiannon was portraying him as the man who didn't care, Kiara knew better. His compassion and kindness had saved her from a darkness that could have swallowed her whole from the moment Adam died. She still hurt. She still ached. But Nick Ruiz had been a friend. A good friend. And even if he was drunk he deserved the same in return. She pressed the doorbell again and was about to knock when the oak door swung back to reveal Nick. She may have been in mourning but she wasn't dead.

The man was sex personified. His jet black hair was slicked back and his eyes were so dark they were almost black. He still wore his slacks, but his coal black, silk shirt hung open revealing a toned body with a mocha tone. The man sent a flush of heat from her neck down to her feet. A small grin tugged at the corners of his mouth. He knew the effect he was having on her and he liked it. A bubble of shame came to the surface that she felt this way. Her reaction to Nick was much different than it had been to Adam. Her love with Adam had been love almost from the start. It was gentle, constant, passionate, and complete. Her response to Nick was something visceral and physical.

"I wasn't sure you'd come."

"I wasn't either."

Nick stepped back from the door.

"Come in. I'm glad you're here."

With great trepidation she entered Nick's home. When he shut the door behind her she jumped. When he locked it she started to panic.

"Look, maybe I should go."

"Please don't go. This house is huge, and with Rhiannon gone," he looked down and steadied his voice, "I just don't want to be alone the first night, you know?"

A lump formed in her throat. Justine and Lynn had stayed with her the first week after Adam had died.

"Yeah I, I know. Is there somewhere I can lay my keys?"

Nick led her into the foyer and then the livingroom. It was dark, with only the moonlight illuminating it. Even with that little light she saw how beautiful the place was. It was champagne on ice and man it was nice to be there.

"I guess you'll want to redesign everything. I on the other hand, want to keep everything the same."

"No, the only room that gives me any trouble is the nursery we designed for the baby. It's the fact that part of my life is gone that's tormenting me right now. Did you want to sit down somewhere?"

"Why do you want me here? I mean you could have gone to any one of the bars and found some company to hash over your divorce with."

Nick stepped close and said in a hushed tone, "Now you know

better than anyone that in my line of work privacy on the home front is important. And I'm just not going to find it in some bar."

Kiara's head spun. It had been two months since she'd been with a man. And Nick Ruiz was a man's man.

"I like you Nick, and you've been there for me. What made you call me?"

"Honestly?" he said touching her hair, "I read Adam's article about you. And I didn't see just a fan. Or even a number one fan. I saw you the way he saw you. The man was hopelessly in love with you. And it's easy to see why."

He trailed her cheek, she pulled back as if he had burned her.

"I'm not the kind of girl who does that sort of thing."

"You've survived a lot, Kiara. Much more pain than I have any right to bitch about. But you have a beauty about you. It comes from a place I don't know that I have. If I have it at all."

Kiara quit thinking about herself and looked into the soul of a man who was aching as much as she was. He did have a strength to him. A passion that would not be denied. It was what drew people to him. And for those that understood him, she was sure it was what made them stay.

"Don't you realize that it was you who didn't run screaming for the hills when I was grieving at the hospital? It takes a special person to stand in the face of that and reach out to the person suffering? And I know how you've been trying to get Jason Dexter out of that ball hog, showboat mentality. And anyone who is as passionate about Kentucky basketball as you are has a heart so strong it can withstand anything. Including an unfaithful wife. And a lost child." Without thinking she laid a comforting hand to his cheek. "You're a good man, Nick Ruiz. And don't you believe anyone who tries to tell you different."

She gazed into his eyes and saw something there she knew she should look away from. That if she didn't look away from it she would be sorry in the end for accepting it.

He took her hand and placed it over his chest.

"You're an amazing woman, Kiara Matthews. I shouldn't have asked you to come over here."

Her breath was leaving her body, her heart racing against

her chest. His touch felt good. His skin was warm and firm beneath her touch. She had the urge to step forward and kiss him. He stroked the top of her hand with his thumb, sending shivers throughout her body, making goosebumps rise on her skin.

"If you want to go I suggest you go now."

Nick's entire manner was that of a wolf's. He looked as if he were about to devour he whole. And she got chills just thinking about it. She wasn't a one night stand kind of girl, but she was aching, and he was hurting and she hadn't been in someone's arms or touched in a long time. He stepped closer, his body inches from hers.

"All that I ask," she said shaking with the need to be touched by Nick, "is that you don't break me."

Before she could take another breath his mouth was on hers and she couldn't breath, she couldn't think, all she could do was feel Nick's lips on hers, and taste the scotch on his expert tongue as he plunged in again and again. Deeper with each stroke until she finally kissed back and a fire lit up her insides as his hands moved down her back and cupped her rear, pressing her close to him. She could feel his excitement at her belly and she sighed into his mouth and wrapped her arms around him, giving into the pleasure that was blotting out the pain.

Pressing her to the wall his hands slipped beneath her t-shirt when his hands reached her bra-less breasts her eyes closed and she moaned.

"Open your eyes, bonita. I want you to see me. I want to see you."

Reaching down he pushed the heel his palm to the softest part between her legs. She tilted her head back and groaned. He began to rub in a fast, hard, rocking motion. It was deft. It was demanding. And she could not do anything but respond to it. And when he bit down on her neck she came. It clouded her brain, it made her body tingle, and it made her knees buckle as she bucked hard against his touch.

"That's right, bonita, come for me. Let it all out. Forget everything else. It's just me and you here and no one else."

Her brain seemed to ride an extra wave of pleasure as he guided her down inside of this game of pretend. This game of there was only the two of them and no one else. For now she could play.

When the orgasm was over she breathed hard, and was transfixed by Nick's hungry stare. He wasn't through with her. Not by a mile. Neither was she.

"Take me to your bed."

He smiled a wolfish grin.

"Are you sure you want to go there?"

Kiara raked his shirt off and threw it off on to the couch. Running her hands over his stomach and chest she held him body to body before running her nails down his back.

"Tell me, Nick Ruiz, are you sure you want to go there?"

She made him so hard he wasn't sure he could wait for the bedroom. And even though he knew this could be wrong. That it could be a mistake. However, he found himself unable to resist the woman who had captured his attention months ago, when she'd grieved as if she were going to die of it.

★★★

They were savage together. Knocking into the dresser. Toppling over lamps, slamming into the armoire. When he suckled at her breasts he left bruises in his wake. And when they kissed they were bruising, punishing, kisses. They fucked on the floor, they fucked against the wall, they even fucked in the shower. And now they were in his bed lost to a savagery only loss and pain could create. She was mounted on top of him, riding him as hard as she could, sweating, her head thrown back, her body clamped to his a tight as she could be. She was hot and wet and slick and she encased him in such away all he could see was her. All he could see was Kiara and her beauty and he wondered how Rhiannon had ever been of interest to him. Because the sex had never been this good with his wife. Ever. He reached up and touched her breasts and she moaned his name. He shivered with pleasure. It had been quite some time since he'd heard his name on Rhiannon's lips.

"Look at me, Kiara."

She looked down and he could tell she was about to climax. It was in the way the fire in her eyes glowed. She tossed her head around, and lifted her arms above her head, then arched her back as she smiled down at him.

"Show off," he said huskily.

She cried out and the sound sent him over the edge and he came harder for her than he'd come for any woman. She collapsed

to him and rolled off of him and laid to his side. He didn't feel
guilty or wrong about sleeping with her. It had felt good, wild,
and without boundaries. Something he only felt when he was
coaching. Something that he was passionate about. And with his
inhibitions down he had given in to a temptation perhaps he
shouldn't have. But he didn't care about that now. He only cared
about being close to Kiara.

Her body, lined with perspiration, glowed next to his. Her
beauty, stunning him. Some people liked lollipops, but he loved a
woman with curves he could feel and fit his body against. And
Kiara was the best example of that. She may have been grieving,
but she bared an animalistic part of her soul to him and she was
laying peaceful at his side.

"I have to go," she said sitting up.

He held on to her.

"What?"

"This was a mistake. I shouldn't have come here and I
shouldn't have done what we just did."

He sat up beside her and touched her face.

"It wasn't wrong, Kiara."

"Adam isn't even cold in his grave. I'm pregnant with his baby. You aren't wrong. For you this is okay. But not for me. Adam was the kind of man you never get over. And by doing this I'm saying I'm over him."

"Listen to me. If what I read about Adam was any indication of what kind of person he was then he wouldn't want you to grieve yourself into the ground with him."

"I wish I knew him as well as you seem to, but I don't so I'm left to my own judgements on this one and I think I messed up in a big way."

His heart fell. He realized he didn't want this to be a mistake. He wanted it to be a little something more.

"If I get a vote I'm glad you cam over tonight. I needed you. I needed a friend."

"You needed a one night stand and I gave in."

He flinched.

"Do you remember the first time we met?"

"You called 911. How could I forget?"

"No, the chapel. Your grief was just so raw and deep. It touched me in a way I have never been touched before. And it's drawn me to you ever since. Even if we're just friends, I don't think I could stand losing you. Please, if this is a mistake, give me a do over. You're UK's Number 1 Fan."

Maybe Adam was there, judging her for moving on so quickly without him. Or maybe he was there, to show her the next step in her life. She loved college basketball. She was fanatical UK basketball. And here was a dashing, sexy, good looking guy who oozed charisma and who half the state's female population would be giving their eye teeth to be in the situation she was in with him. She closed her eyes and the image of Adam gazing down into her eyes in the hospital. No, he would never judge her. For any reason. She had come to Nick's knowing full well what might happen. And she was wrestling with whether or not she wanted her life to continue down any path with him at all. The sex had been hot. A fiery, all consuming kind of thing. And if she were honest with herself she wanted more of it. But did Nick? Then she felt it. A gentle touch of flesh to her lips by his. Then his forehead to hers.

"Tell me you don't want to go. That you want to stay."

"You have to promise me one thing."

"Anything."

"That I have to die before you do."

"Why?"

"Because I can't do it again."

"I can't promise that."

"Why not?"

"Because I want to believe I can be a better man."

Kiara held his face in her hands.

"You are a better man, Nick. You are..."

He kissed her slow, but with the same kind of intensity that was breaking her resolve. Laying her back to the bed he parted her legs and situated himself between them. He raked his gaze over her body and smiled.

"Beauty personified. Grace personified. Integrity personified. I only hope I can prove myself worthy of what I know of you."

He lifted her bottom up with his hands and placed his face between her legs. A delicious ache shot through her sex and her body, jolting Kiara into another world. As his tongue licked her, his teeth nibbled her, and his mouth coaxed her, her body felt a frenzied need as his tongue stroked over her sex and plunged inside her, again and again. She began to rock to the gentle rythm he set, touching her, loving her, making her think of the future will acknowledging the past. He concentrated on her sex, laving it pounding it with tongue until she might go mad with the anticipation of coming. Finally she came, the sensation of pleasurable ache crashing down over her, washing away the pain, and guilt, and years of shame. She thought of Adam, of their daughter waiting to be born. Every part of her soul shattered as she fell back to the earth and into the present.

Nick kissed her belly, her chest, her lips, and took her in his arms. She started quietly at first, but as her shoulders shook he held her close and murmured in her ear.

"It's okay, bonita. I'm here. For you. I'm here for you." He kissed her temple. When she clung to him it surprised him, but it was the most natural thing in the world for him to tighten his hold.

Chapter Fifteen

Jason Dexter watched as the people from Sports Illustrated set up the shoot for coach Ruiz's girlfriend, and he didn't like it. That should be him representing the Wildcats. This bitch was just a fan. A crazy one at that. She'd been to a couple of practices, sitting quietly in the stands, watching the team, watching the coach, watching him with a stern, intense stare. As if he didn't deserve to wear the jersey of a Kentucky Wildcat. Big Blue Nation his ass. They were just a bunch of crazy fucks.

They should get down on their hands and knees and kiss his ass for coming to their precious school at all.

A tall, muscular man came through with a man dressed in a business suit. He was sharp, slick. He had to be connected to Sports Illustrated. The muscular guy had to be his bodyguard.

"Alright, everybody in their places. She's coming to set now."

The woman representing UK fans everywhere didn't look happy. She looked nervous. She wore an oversized jersey bearing the number one and home colors of white and blue. Who christened her No. 1? And who said a fan scores a place in the most important sports magazine instead of him, or any other UK player.

She looked up and stared at him. A chill went down his spine. There was something there, a toughness he hadn't counted on. A sadness that angered him. Who was she to ask for pity or put on a show?

"Thomas I'm not sure this is a good idea, can't you just run the article?"

"You're the star of the story. I have to run it with your photograph."

"I don't photograph well."

"Are you kidding me? Adam thought you were beautiful. He would have insisted on you at least being in the picture if he knew he was getting the byline."

"You flatter me."

"I try. This is Haven, he's your bodyguard. Nick insisted that you have one."

"Why?"

Thomas looked over at Jason. Jason pretended not to notice.

"Do you really want to get into that around here?"

"My life has been splashed across the news for the past year. Do you think I care if everyone here knows my life story?"

"Calm down. Nick knows the shooter is still out there. And he doesn't want them to get a hold of you and finish the job they started with Adam."

"There were others shot and injured that night. I didn't even get a good look at the gunman," she lowered her head, "I didn't get the chance to."

Jason jumped in with his opinion. Unasked for. Unwanted. And without any tact.

"Coach needs to get this lady out of here. I ain't gettin'
shot for nobody."

"Who is this kid?" Thomas asked.

"Who is this kid? I'm the best player on this team. That's
who this kid is."

A snarl of contempt lit up Kiara's face.

"Who is this kid? A talented, overrated, selfish, ball hog
who refuses to listen to his coach. That's who Jason Dexter is."

He was shocked that anyone dared to say those things to him.
And when she came at him he didn't know quite what to do. So when
the heel of her palm pummeled the bottom of his nose his eyes
teared and blood began to gush from his nose.

Haven was between them before she could do anymore damage
than she already had. Not that she didn't try. But Haven was too
strong for her. The blood pounded in her ears. She tasted blood.
She couldn't stand this kid. He was a snot. A showboat. An
ingrate. And Nick was giving him chance, after chance, after
chance, and still he bucked the system. Tubby had had the same
problem with him. Maybe it wasn't the coach. Maybe it was the
kid. No matter how one looked at it this kid was spitting in the

face of an opportunity most kids didn't have a prayer of getting.

"Get that crazy bitch away from me. Get her away before I kick her ass."

"Try it with a broken nose. I dare you. Just try it!"

"What the hell is going on in here?"

Nick.

"She broke my nose Coach."

"All right, all right. Alicia! We've got blood."

The feeling of rage which had coursed through her body so easily subsided. Nick wasn't the sweet understanding man Adam was. He would want answers. And if he didn't like them he might get rid of her. That would be something she had to live with. She wasn't going to cry about it. It wasn't something to be cried over. A tall, sleek, woman came through and put on a pair of latex gloves and began examining Jason.

With his hands on his hips Nick turned to her and softened.

"What happened?"

"We just rubbed each other the wrong way. He doesn't like the fact that I'm here. And I don't like the way he's squandering his opportunity to play for the Wildcats."

"Why'd you hit him?"

"Because of his arrogant mistreatment of the SI staff. Because of his arrogance period."

Nick smiled.

"Bonita, you can't go around fighting everyone who pisses you off. It's not good for business."

The smile disappeared as he turned to Jason.

"Is it broken?"

Alicia shoved gauze into his nose.

"No, but she got him pretty good. His just needs to keep it clean for the next couple of days. And I'd bench him if I were you for the next few practices."

"See what that bitch did?"

A blaze of anger went through Nick's entire being. He got into Jason's face. And a roar so loud echoed in the room it reverberated off the walls filled the room.

"You will respect her! You will do it when I'm in room or when I'm not! For that I'm not just going to bench you for a couple of practices I'm going to bench you for the first two games! So until you can get with it you're going to be watching film with me! Understand!"

Jason refused to meet Nick's gaze.

"Look at me," Nick hissed, "I said, look-at-me."

Finally Jason looked at his coach. Coach wanted to be there. Coach wanted him there. But he wasn't going to take his shit anymore. Funny that it took a woman to make him see that. A woman who had attacked him no less.

Nick could see it. This incident had gotten through to Jason. Now he had to make sure that the lesson stuck. Without Kiara getting involved.

"C'mon, let's go look at some film."

"Actually, Coach. I'd like to stay in here. That is, if Miss Matthews doesn't mind."

She smiled wryly.

"No, Jason. I don't mind."

"Okay people, let's get this going. Time is money," Thomas shouted.

The photographer, a very attractive British man smiled and directed Kiara to the chair.

"Dear if you'll just straddle the chair we can get started.

That's right, there you go. Now just tilt your head and smile. That's good. Now turn a little."

As the camera clicked, and flashes popped, Kiara thought of Adam's article. She thought of how Thomas made it happen. And she smiled at the thought of the feel of Nick's arms wrapped around her. And taste of his kisses. If she had hit the jackpot with Adam, he was looking down on her, and sending her a dream to heal her heart.

***

It was late. Kiara knew not to expect Nick so close to Midnight Madness, but it was hard not to. Their sex was such that it made her long for more of him. It wasn't like she loved him or anything. It was too soon after Adam. But she didn't mind being referred to as the mystery woman in Nick's life. Stroking Chyna's fur, Kiara relished the purring sound she made at being so close to her owner.

Chyna was a life saver. Anytime she felt lonely or like she couldn't go on, her orange tabby appeared out of nowhere and leapt up on to her lap and kneaded her stomach, purring loud and strong. Kiara loved her kitty cat. And even though both Crispa and Adam had been strictly against it Kiara would sneak table scraps to Chyna. And Chyna loved her for it.

The first game of Kentucky's 1995-96 season was playing, but Kiara wasn't paying attention to it. She was waiting for the knock at the door that would signal either Nick's arrival or that dinner was ready. Thank God there was a Chinese food restaurant that delivered not that far away from where she lived. She bent over and kissed Chyna on top of her furry little head and continued to pet her. She was her final link to Crispa. Much like the baby she carried was her last link to Adam. A soft knock at the door broke her from her thoughts. Didn't sound like the delivery guy. Nick had never been to her house. With what they tended to do when they got together it didn't feel right doing it there. Another soft knock followed by a, "Hey there, it's Nick."

His accent sent shivers down her spine. Nick made her feel sensual and sexual all over. And it was okay. Adam had made it possible for her to do those things. A twinge of sadness forced a lump up her throat. If things had been different...who knew. Right now she was in he midst of an affair with a man who had been there the day it had all fallen apart. He was the one who understood. The one who was there for her. She felt alive when she was with him. And she could make her memories with Adam about more than the awful night he died. She could make them stop for what was just a little while. Another soft knock.

"Are you okay in there?"

She opened the door up and smiled. His arms were loaded up with dinner.

"I caught the delivery guy. My treat."

Kiara shook her head.

"No, no. I bought the food. I'll pay for it."

"Kiara," he tried to insist.

"Hey, you're my guest. We'll do what I want."

"I thought if I was a guest we did what I wanted to do."

"Get in here and shut the God damn door. And don't forget to lock it. I'll get some plates. I hope you like shrimp, chicken, and beef, because I got fried rice and the triple delight."

"Generally speaking I don't eat Chinese, too much fat and msg. But for you I'll make an exception."

She threw her head back and laughed. A loud, full throated laugh. Nick liked it when Kiara laughed, she didn't do it often, but when she did it was like a beautiful array of colors lighting up her face. The best time was when she came, her face glowed and she would gaze into his eyes. It was...it was enough to make him forget the fact she'd almost broken his best, if not inconsistent player's nose. He walked over to her and kissed her, and tasted her tongue with his own. She froze momentarily then kissed him back.

"I'm not here to replace Adam, you know that don't you?"

Without looking at him she nodded her head yes and gave a weak, "Yeah," as a reply.

Nick knew he would have to be patient, and he was willing to give it a go, but he wasn't known for his patience. But Kiara was unlike any woman he'd ever known or loved. And he could love her. His feelings were such that maybe that could happen.

"Hey," he said softly, "I'm here to be Nick Ruiz. I'm here to be here for you. And care about you. And make you feel like the kind of woman I think you are. The woman you already were. So don't cop out on me. Not now."

"This is my home. This was mine and Adam's home. I had a future planned with him. We had a future planned together. It's just hard for me to imagine another life here. Another man. Another anything. And, as much as I like you, I'm finding the transition hard when I'm here."

"Come here."

He held his arm out. She hesitated. He stepped closer and pulled her to his chest.

"I'm willing to take this as fast or as slow as you want it to go. All I ask is that you don't shut me out. And that you give me a chance."

"Oh, is that all," she said with a small smile.

"That, and you keep your hands off my players. I can get fired over incidents like it."

She shook her head.

"I don't know what's wrong with me."

"You're grieving, angel. And basketball is your outlet. And to be honest with you, I think you finally did what I couldn't. You got through to him."

"By giving him a nose bleed?"

"By showing him he wasn't the hotshot he thought he was."

She wrapped her arms around Nick, and rested her head to his chest. He smelled good. Like Obsession for Men and soap. She was sorry for making things so hard on him. But that shooter had made things impossible for her and Nick was the man stepping up to the challenge.

"Hold me. Please. Just hold me."

Nick held her close and breathed in her scent of soap and shampoo. He found himself thinking he could stand there with her in the kitchen forever. Adam may have been her angel, but as he radiated in her warmth, and strength, and vulnerability, he realized, he had discovered his.

Chapter Sixteen

The crowd was raucous and roaring in Rupp Arena for the game against the University of Louisville. It was New Year's Eve and Kiara was decked out in a maternity sized blue and white sweater She also had the emblem UK painted on her cheeks. Nick had her team on a good run so far. With wins over Indiana and North Carolina he had already set the expectations high. And now that he was tangoing with former mentor Pitino he was holding his own before a large crowd of 24,000 plus fans. And for the first time in her college ball obsessed life she was waving a pom pom and screaming her lungs out, live, at a UK/U of L game. The only other time she'd been privy to such excitement and joy when it came to basketball was when she and Crista had attended the Duke/UK match-up shortly before Crista had died.

As she watched Jason run the floor she smiled. He'd become quite the little floor general in the last three months. One brush with her temper had been enough for him. However, in order to get him to stay and bribe the media into secrecy, she was banned from practices altogether. Which was a shame, she really liked watching her team learning how to do what any UK team did. Learning how to stomp a mud hole in anyone's ass who dared step up to their excellence. And she got a high off of watching Nick coach his boys with a relish and a passion that matched her own. They'd spent many a night pouring over film of other teams into the wee hours of the morning. The night before the UofL game had been the most intense yet. With her playing hostess to a gaggle of assistants and strength trainers all while watching intently in the background. And she'd witnessed something on the tape. A Pitino tell that could work in the Wildcats favor. Something that if capitalized on would secure them a key win, and signal a resurgence in the program. But she was not a coach. She was Nick's mystery woman. She didn't even rank as high as a girlfriend. So she assumed they would catch it and left it at that.

But as the Cardinals scored basket after basket, and ratcheted up the intensity each trip up the court, Kiara stood up, her seven month belly protruding and began to make her way down to the bench.

Nick was coaching them as hard as he could. His boys weren't under performing, the Cardinals were just that much quicker down the court, just that much faster off the dribble, and just that much better all around. He'd known that this would be a tough game going in, but he'd made his boys believe that they could win against this caliber of talent, against a coach who was just as good, if not better than he was. He looked at the clock. 5:45 remaining. He looked at the score. 73-60. Not in their favor. He was about to call a time out when his assistant tapped him on the shoulder, "Coach, I think you'll want to hear this."

He turned around. Kiara was standing there with his dry erase board.

"Is it the baby?"

"No. It's this."

She started diagraming the game. Immediately he turned to his assistant. He was angry.

"Get her out of here."

"Coach."

"I said get her out of here."

"*Coach.*"

"I said get her the fuck out of here!"

Kiara froze. She knew she had over stepped her boundaries. But no one talked to her like that. Not anymore. Her blood ran hot as she struggled to maintain her composure. She completed the diagram and thrust it into the assistant's hands.

"Tell him to shove it up his ass for all I care. And that if he wants me to disappear there are much classier ways to do it."

Fighting back the rage she was feeling, Kiara made a hasty retreat out of Rupp Arena. She didn't bother to look back to see Nick examining her play.

"Go get her."

"Coach, you didn't see what I saw. She ain't coming back."

"What did I say?"

"Sorry. No can do. I told you what she said. I am not facing it again."

"Damn it Clyde! She's on to something here and your wasting our time if you don't go get her."

"Five minutes isn't going to soothe a pregnant woman's hurt feelings. You of all people should know that."

Nick's eyes were dark anyway, Clyde watched as they turned black.

"If we lose this game I'm going to make you run laps. Time out!"

Nick gathered his boys around, and continued to examine the

play. What was the word Adam had used in the SI article? Savant. The woman he had been sharing a life with for the last three months was a college basketball savant. She had figured out what was holding his boys back, while ferreting out his former mentor's weaknesses. He felt like a total ass for yelling at her like she wasn't even there. But this wasn't the time to kick himself. There was under four minutes to play and his team needed him to be a man about it and coach them. And if Kiara was indeed Big Blue Nation's number one fan, she would understand, and if he was trying to be the better man she believed him to be he would go to her as soon as the buzzer sounded. No matter what the final score was.

***

Nick unlocked the door to Kiara's home and searched for her. Only to find her in the living room, sitting a few feet from the television watching a video he had never seen before. In it she was smiling and laughing and next to her was Adam holding her around the waist, laughing right along with her.

"We won."

"I saw the news. We're all over it. Local. National. ESPN.

I'm sorry I made such an ass of myself, Nick. You're the coach.
I'm not on your staff. I had no business coming up to you the way
I did."

Her body was sagging, curled in, and her back was to his
gaze. It was his turn to try and smooth things out.

"I shouldn't have talked to you the way I did. Maybe you
shouldn't have come to me the way you did, but there's a much
better way to take care of a situation like that. Besides,
without your scouting we wouldn't have won."

"So where does that leave us?"

"What are you talking about?"

"I miss him, Nick. At night, when I'm alone, I'm sick with
it. I think, Crista will never know her father, or what he gave
up so that she could be born. And then there's the time I'm with
you. You take away the hurt, and the misery, and the ache of it
all and I think, maybe I can go on. Then today happens, and I
think, what the hell am I thinking. How can I possibly fall in
love with another man when I'm still grieving the man who gave me
my life back."

"I'll never be able to replace Adam. He was too good a

person. Too kind. Too patient. Too compassionate for a man like me with too many flaws, and too much anger to do something like that. But I can be the man who loves you. Is there for you, and promise my heart to no other. I would never dare try to replace the man on that screen."

A burst of laughter, Adam's laughter, kept Kiara's attention on the screen.

"He was beautiful."

Nick watched the screen and how Adam gazed at Kiara. He was beautiful. And it was clear how much he loved her. Nick felt a pang of jealousy. He wanted Kiara to bask in his gaze like that. To know how deep his feelings were beginning to run.

"Of course he was."

"He thought I was beautiful."

"Of course he did."

"He didn't believe I was damaged goods. He made me believe I could get better."

"Why wouldn't he?"

She lowered her head and turned around, finally facing him.

"I loved him, Nick. He was my everything. And as hard as I

try I can't stop from loving him as if he were here."

He went to her and took her in his arms.

"He will always be your everything. He left you his and your child. He will always be here. And any time you miss him too much, put in any tape with him on it, or any of the countless UK games you watched together. I know it will hurt, but he'll be here. He'll always be here. And there's nothing wrong with that."

She peered up at him, pain etching its way across her face.

"Then how come I have to feel so guilty about falling in love with you?"

He thought he might crush her to his chest in that moment. Over the last three months they had danced around each other. Making love, having sex, exchanging keys, developing a friendship, and it all came to a head at the game. She did something a friend would do. Something a coach would do. Something only a lover would dare to do. Only something a woman like Kiara Matthews would do.

"It's okay to feel guilty. It's normal to feel guilty with what you've experienced. But know, you don't have to. Not with me. Because I'll never try to replace Adam Paul Matthews. I'll just love you the best way Nick Ruiz can."

"Kiss me, Nick."

He hesitated. He did not want a repeat of their first night together. He wanted this to mean more than that. He wanted it to mark the beginning of something new.

"Just kiss me, Nick. Before I change my mind."

And kiss her he did. There was something in the way that he kissed her, in the way he swept her up in his embrace he carried her away with the touch of his lips. It wasn't like it was with Adam. With Adam it was like the fairy tale. The storybook. With Nick it was like On the Road with Jack Kerouac. Or the Saturns of Titan by Kurt Vonnegut. It was full of passion and rock and roll, and the rhythm of a great basketball game. And when he finally broke the kiss they were breathing hard and panting. She was tasting her lips with her tongue and touching his lower lip with her finger. She smiled. He caressed her cheek with his thumb.

"Do you know how gorgeous you are?"

"Sometimes. When Adam looked at me a certain way. Or you kiss me like you just did. It lets me know, that, there are men. Successful, sexy, passionate men like yourself who find women, like me, attractive."

He took her face in his hands and gazed down at her with such a fierce intensity it sent a tremble straight to her core, causing her to shake with anticipation.

"Bonita, you have to believe it for yourself. I know life has treated you terribly, but despite the evil that lurks in your past, I'm here. And I couldn't have asked for a better chance at love than having you in my life. It's terrible what brought you here to me. And Adam will always be your angel. But you bonita, you will always be mine."

Kiara smiled again.

"You and Adam have one thing in common."

"What's that?"

"Words that make it all better."

She looked at him and felt her heart drop into her stomach and do flips. He wanted her. A man who shared her passion for the Wildcats of Kentucky, and college basketball, and national championships wanted her. The man on People's Sexiest Men Alive list wanted her. The man who had helped her through the worst of it, the man who had stuck by her even when she pushed him away

was there standing by her now. Wanting her now. She had lost
Crista, her best friend. She had lost Adam Paul Matthews the love
of her life, and the father of their child. Dare she take a
chance and love the man before her now? The man who had showed
her his temper, yet had come to her for forgiveness? Even when
she had been crazy enough to up and try to tell him how to coach
his team. Big Blue Nation's team?

"Make me a scout."

"That isn't very romantic."

"Yes it is. It's the most romantic thing I can think of
right now."

Nick could see it. She loved him. It was right there in the
way she looked at him. But she loved UK basketball as much, if
not more. And she needed to love him as much, if not more than
her greatest passion of all. And to be connected to him, would be
to be connected to the sport, that in a way, bound them together
from the very beginning. Something different than him watching
her, watch Adam die. The diagram proved she had more than just a
passion for the game, that she had an eye and a brain for it as
well.

"Okay. On a trial run. You can watch film with me and the other coaches and take notes. I fully expect you to be at every game on the bench. I don't know how I'm going to do it, but I'll try to get Mitch to agree to it. And I'll have to explain it to the boys. Don't be too surprised if this is met with some resistance. You're a woman. And a lot people see this as a man's game, but with Adam's article running next week, it should make my job a little bit easier."

"The article runs next week?"

"Yes. And guess who's on the cover."

She was stunned. Sports Illustrated wasn't necessarily a bastion of UK support. When the 1989 scandal broke they had put Kentucky on the cover all right. The words 'Kentucky's Shame' were burned into the Big Blue Nation's collective conscience. She was going to be on the cover? She, representing Adam's one and only big time byline, would be presented to the sports would as Big Blue Nation's number one fan? She could only hope to do Adam's words proud. She didn't know whether to kiss Nick, or start to cry.

"Are you going to say something, Kiara? It is a good thing

they're running the article isn't it?"

She nodded her head and started to grin, a joy lighting her up the way he loved best. Adam must have seen it in her too. It was too obvious to miss. She pulled him into a soft, sensuous, kiss.

"Thank you, Nick."

"For what, bonita?"

"For letting me grieve. For letting me love Adam, for giving me the space to love you. Because, as much as I miss him, I think I could love you just as much, but in a different way."

"Angel, you make it easy."

"I love you, Nick. With all of my heart. I love you."

"I love you, my angel, my bonita. Let me show you," he said pulling her sweater over her head and tossing it aside.

"Just one thing first."

She grabbed the remote and turned the television off.

"I don't want to share this moment with anyone."

Then she laid a kiss on him that said you belong to me and nobody else. All he could do was let her take the lead, and when she stood and held out her hand, and gazed down at him, he saw

the love and heat. She was taking him the one place they had
never been to in her house. The bedroom. He took her hand.
Tonight was the celebration of what he had never experienced
before. A woman who knew him. A woman who understood him. A woman
who got him. A woman he could truly love. A woman who would never
leave him. A woman he would never leave.

Chapter Seventeen

Kiara smiled at the feeling of warmth she had both inside and out. Being spooned by Nick with his hand at her naked, pregnant, belly felt natural. They had been intimate the night before. But it was in a much different way than in the past. Adam wasn't in the room with her, he was nestled in her heart, in a place where no one could touch.

Nicked snuggled against her, and buried his face in at the nape of her neck. He skin felt good next to hers and she wished they could lay there forever. He kissed her below her ear and groaned.

"I have to go to work, bonita."

She flushed from her head to her feet, and tugged his arm up around her chest.

"Stay. For just a few minutes. Then go. I know you have a job to go to, but this is nice. I haven't had it in a long time."

When Rhiannon had been pregnant this had been a source of contention. But now, with Kiara, a few minutes was okay. It made him feel like a better man to do it. And if anyone deserved to be loved by a better man, Kiara did.

"Nick, can I ask you something?"

"You can ask me anything."

"And you promise not to get angry."

"That depends on what you ask me."

She took a deep breath and counted to ten.

"Bonita?"

"Okay, I just had to get my nerve up," she managed to roll over and sit up.

Nick looked up at her and she felt like the most beautiful girl in the world. In the past she would cover her body, even with Adam for a long time. But beneath Nick's loving gaze it felt natural to be naked and not shield her skin from him.

"Get your nerve up about what?"

"What went wrong with you and Rhiannon? She came from a basketball family, and you were a product of Pitino's mentoring. I suppose to me that's the storybook."

Nick sighed. She'd opened up about her pain and her grief, but his had only been mentioned in passing. He wasn't keen on doing it now. But she was coming to him with an open heart, and if he were honest, while Rhiannon may have been unfaithful, it had been a mismatch from the start.

"She wanted something different from me. She wanted a husband who worked nine to five and could be there for her when she needed him to be. Hell, I even missed what I believed to be the birth of our child because of the kind of person I am."

Kiara's face darkened.

"You stopped for me that day."

"Oh, angel. I didn't mean it like that."

"Then how did you mean it?"

"That if I had been there for her in the past, maybe she wouldn't have cheated, and maybe we would've stayed together. Or maybe she would've seen me for the man that I was and steered clear of me. All I know, is since the moment I met you I've been a different man. A better man."

"I've got news for you. You've always been a better man. You stopped to help two people you didn't even know. You paid his medical expenses. And you helped me to believe in me, and in life when I thought for sure God had abandoned me for good."

He reached up and ran his fingers through her hair.

"I don't know about God, but Kiara, I'll never leave your side."

She smiled and kissed his fingertips.

"I'd kiss your lips, but Crista might have something to say about that."

Nick laid his palm to her stomach and both of them jumped.

"She either really likes me or she really hates me."

About that time both of them felt her kick again. Kiara covered Nick's hand with her own.

"There's something I wanted to ask you other than about Rhiannon."

He felt Crista move again. It made his heart jump. Being a father, he hadn't realized how hurt he was when Rhiannon had so unceremoniously yanked his heart out of his chest the way that she had when she'd announce the child she held in her arms was not theirs. But now, as he felt Crista moving beneath his palm he had hope. Hope for a future he hadn't known that he would have the day his life had fallen apart.

"Nick."

"Yes?"

"Did you hear what I said?"

"I'm sorry. Say at it again."

"I said, there's something else I wanted to ask, but I think the mood has passed."

Kiara tried to get out of bed, but he squeezed her hand.

"Kiara, don't let me spoil the mood. I want to look forward to watching film with you later, not worrying whether or not we're going to fight because I did something stupid."

"Well, it's the baby's name."

"What about it?"

"I want it to be Crista Fellows Ruiz-Matthews."

Nick sat straight up and blinked, he didn't know what to say. He hadn't seen that coming. Give the child his name, she was still wearing the ring Adam gave her and he, even though he knew a little girl was coming into this world, hadn't really thought about being a dad again until he placed his palm to her belly moments ago. He wanted to say yes, but did he a right to?

"Have you thought about this? Adam and Crista, those are important people in your life, I'm just the man who loves you."

Tears glistened in her eyes.

"Just the man who loves me? Don't you know you're so much more than that to me? You're my best friend, you're my soulmate, You're the whole package Nick. After last night I knew that God hadn't abandoned me at all. That even though Crispa had indeed been my best friend. And that Adam will always live on through little Crista, all the pain, all the joy, it's brought me to you. You're the only one I know who loves UK basketball as much as I do. The only one who'll even look at me like I'm the only woman in the room, and I can tell you anything and you won't judge me for it."

Best friend. Soulmate. Was she saying she wanted a lifetime with him? A man like him? Was he the better man she deserved? He drew her back against him.

"I had no idea you felt so strongly about us."

"I told you I loved you. Were you telling me the truth when you said you loved me?"

"Yes."

"Then why are you acting so funny now?"

Her body was tense against his. Stress could not be good for the baby. And with the kind of stress Kiara had been under from the start hadn't been good. He did love her. He was afraid he didn't deserve her.

"I'm not the better man you think I am. I've done a lot of shitty things to he women in my life."

"Have you hit them?"

"No."

"Have you verbally abused them?"

"No."

"Ever raped them?"

"God no."

"Then what could you have done that was so bad that would make you not the better man?"

"I chose basketball over them at every turn. And I just expected them to like it."

She took his hands and pressed them to her stomach.

"They knew what they were getting into when they met you. I don't feel sorry for them."

"I'm not perfect, angel."

"Neither am I. But you love me anyway, right?"

"Right."

Kiara held out her hands and looked down at them. Adam's ring staring back at her.

"I think it's time this moved to a gold chain, don't you?" she said removing the engagement ring.

Nick couldn't believe it. She was really taking huge steps. She had so much faith in him, did he have the guts to back what she was so sure of.

"I'm a rotten husband, a rotten fiancé, and a rotten boyfriend. I will choose the job over you every time. I'll break your heart. But if you'll have me, I'll love you for the rest of our lives."

Kiara burst into laughter as she sat the ring on the night stand next to her bed. She twisted around and smiled wide and bright.

"That, without a doubt is the strangest, weirdest, most honest proposal I've ever heard. And if you'll have me, I'll prove to you just how wrong you are about yourself."

She was so breathtaking, nude, with child, and in his arms. He wanted to make her his forever, and there was only one way to do that.

"Marry me."

"Come again?"

"Marry me."

"You want to marry me?"

"Why wouldn't I want to marry you?"

Kiara picked the ring back up and pang of sadness went through her over what might have been.

"Would you mind if I wore this ring on my other hand?"

"I insist that you do it."

She slid the ring on her right hand, flexed it and smiled. She turned and faced him.

"Yes, Nick Ruiz, I'll marry you. I'll marry you because I love you for who you are. I'll marry you because you've helped heal my heart. And I'll marry you because you're the better man."

He kissed her, sweeping her up in his arms, and felt himself grow hard at her response. She must have too, because when they broke the kiss she smiled.

"You better go to work before I make you late," she said leaning him back.

"Oh, I think they can wait a few minutes for me."

"Oh, they can, can they? I sure hope so, because when I get through with you you're going to need all the time you can get to go to work."

He arched his eyebrows.

"Just remember. When I get back we're going to Vegas. So you better be sure you want to sap me of all my strength."

"Don't worry about me. I've already got that taken care of. You just lay back and enjoy."

As he laid down, she kissed him down his chest, nipping at his skin until she took him in her mouth, and light turned to pleasure. And all he could see was her, him, and little Crispa in a bright, bright, future.

***

"You're getting what?!" Helen shouted, blowing a whole through her eardrum.

She and Kiara were sitting in her kitchen having lunch. It was something they had taken to doing to get through the hard part of losing Adam. It was what brought them together, and it seemed by the tone in her voice what could, tear them apart.

"Please, Helen, you knew I was seeing Nick."

"Yes, but I had no idea just how serious it was."

"The fact I'm marrying Nick doesn't mean I don't love Adam anymore. And it doesn't have to mean you're not a part of my life from here on end either. You and Michael have been the best parents I could've asked for, the baby I'm carrying is your grandchild."

Helen's lips were pursed together. It was clear she was unhappy and did not approve.

"How well do you actually know this man?"

"As well as I knew Adam when he proposed. Nick loves me. Our relationship dynamic is different than the one I had with Adam, but I love him. And he understands me and I understand him. I'm getting another shot at happiness here. And I want you to be happy for me. You and Michael. You're an important part of my life."

Helen set down her glass of tea and leaned back in her chair.

"Over the last year I've gotten to know you Kiara. And I've gotten to see what it is Adam saw in you that drew him to you so quickly. You weren't what I thought of as his type."

"Petite, thin, blonde?"

Helen had the decency to look ashamed of herself.

"I was wrong. I see what Adam saw now. You're smart, funny, pretty, and passionate. I see why other men would fall in love with you. But it seems so soon. Almost too soon. How can you be sure that it's what you want?"

"Because he wants to be a better man. Because he is a better man. Adam was the perfect man. And he will always be here," Kiara said rubbing her stomach, "but Nick, the only thing he has in common with Adam is that he loves me, and would do anything for me. I will never find another Adam. I don't want another Adam. I want Nick. Please say you'll drive with us to Las Vegas tonight. You and Michael both. His mother and father are going to meet us there. I'd really like to have you there as the family I never had."

Helen's features softened a bit.

"I miss my son."

"I miss him too. And this is how I've gotten through. But you're his mother, there's nothing like that kind of love. She's not even here and I can't imagine losing Crista. It wouldn't just be losing a child it would be like losing Adam all over again. And that I don't think I can bear the thought of. So, if you don't feel like you can come, then don't, but please, don't cut us out of your life. It keeps Adam close, even though he's not here with me anymore."

Helen sighed and a smile tugged at the corners of her mouth.

"So is the sex good?"

"Let's just say, the boy knows what he's doing."

Helen laughed. Then measured Kiara up.

"Adam loved you. And I don't think he would want me to stand in the way of your happiness. So yes, Michael and I will pack up and meet you back here, say? Five o'clock?"

"You should probably get dinner before you come over. Nick works long hours. Better make it seven or eight."

Helen drained her glass and picked up her purse. She walked over to Kiara and kissed her on the cheek.

"You're going to make a lovely bride. I hope Adam will be

able to see it. Wherever he's at."

Tears sprang to Kiara's eyes.

"I hope so too Helen. Now go before you make me cry."

After Helen left, Kiara lowered her head and began to cry. Not out of guilt. But out of acknowledging, for the first time in five months, that Adam had indeed loved her so much that he made his family fall in love with her too.

Chapter Eighteen

Justine was helping her with the last minute shopping.
Including the dress.

"I suppose white is out," Kiara said looking through a
specialty maternity rack.

Justine laughed.

"You'll be gorgeous in anything you wear. Why don't you try
this one on."

It was a beautiful gown. Diaphanous, silky, and satiny, the
white and light silver dress looked great on the hanger. The
question was, would it look great on her. Snatching it out of

Justine's hands Kiara headed for the dressing room.

"I've already tried on ten different dresses. This had better be the one."

"It will be. Trust me."

Kiara closed the door and slipped out of her clothes and into the dress. It fit her perfectly. She rubbed her eyes. Dare she say it, dare she even think it. She liked the way it looked on her. It was comfortable, it was pretty, and it shimmered. She shimmered. She hoped she did at least.

"Justine," she called out as she pulled back the curtain, "what do you think?"

"Oh Kiara. You're beautiful. If I wasn't dating Lynn, and you were a lesbian I'd so marry you."

Both of them let out peals of laughter.

"It really looks that good?"

"If he ain't in love with you now, he will be when he sees you in this dress."

"Thank God that's over with. Now all I've got to do is find the shoes and were done. Are you sure you and Lynn can't come?"

Justine gave her a winsome look.

"I'd really, really, like to come, but Adam's replacement is a real hard ass who doesn't have a Kiara at home to win over his heart."

A soft ache went through Kiara's heart.

"You think he sees this and approves?"

"I think he sees everything and approves. Now come on, let's buy the dress and get the hell out of here."

Kiara slipped back into the dressing room and looked at herself, then touched her belly. Nick loved her. Nick understood her. And Nick was making room in his heart for her. As she gazed into the mirror she thought of his body next to hers. Of how he kissed her and how they had made love just that morning. She loved him. Was in love with him. Would spend the rest of her life with him. She looked upwards and whispered, "Thank you, Adam. Thank you."

***

"Oh miha, you look so beautiful. My Nick is going to fall in love with you all over again."

Bella Ruiz looked Kiara up and down in the back of the little chapel in Las Vegas. Her husband, Antonio was standing at the altar with his son waiting for Kiara to join him. Helen was in complete agreement.

"Oh yes, you and Justine picked out the perfect dress. You're glowing. And the white roses are from me and Michael. I know losing Adam was just as hard on you as was on me. But it's so clear that he loves you and that you love him. You should see him, he's so nervous it's cute."

"He's nervous? I'm the one who's shaking and fiending for frickled pickles and horseradish sauce."

"How sweet. There's no need to be nervous, dear. You're going to be with the man you love. It's one of the most wonderful moments you'll ever remember."

The music started to play.

"Just remember miha, my Nick loves you. He must, after being burned by that puta I didn't think he'd ever even want to marry again. But you gave him hope. And I'll never forget that. Now go to him. He's waiting."

Kiara turned to Helen who had tears in her eyes.

"Go to him, Kiara. It's what I believe Adam would have wanted if he knew how heartbroken you'd been. He would never have left you alone. He sent Nick to you. I believe it. Go. Before you make me cry."

Bella and Helen rushed to their seats and as Kiara appeared at the back and revealed herself she saw Nick and Nick saw her and it was magical.

Nick felt his heart race and his stomach flip. She was lit up from the inside out and glowed an array of different colors. A spectrum of lights crossed her features and he realized just how lucky he was to have found her at all and he couldn't wait to not only declare his love for her, but promise to love, protect, honor, and cherish her for as long as they both lived.

As she reached him and stood beside him, Kiara felt a well of emotion bubble up inside her and she didn't know she could feel this way. So much joy and love and hope, without the fear of it being yanked away from her was new to her and it was hard to contain it.

The good Reverend Richardson stood before them with a bible in his hands. But they were in Las Vegas so things were a little unconventional.

"Nick Ruiz and Kiara Matthews I understand you have written

your own vows."

"Yes Reverend, we have."

"Well, usually I would read a little from the bible and guide the bride and groom through a little lesson about the type of commitment they were about to make. But Mr. Matthews and Mr. Ruiz came to me before their children arrived tonight and told me their story. I was so touched and moved by their story that I figured I had learned the lesson and that all that was left for Nick and Kiara to do was recite their vows to one another. So Kiara, you may speak what it is that is in your heart."

Kiara handed off her bouquet of white roses to Helen and turned to Nick and took his hands in hers. She gazed up into his eyes and knew that this marked the beginning of something new. A journey that would take them far in to the future. So when she spoke, speaking her heart was what she did.

"My life has been a series of dark moments punctuated by moments of streams of light. Only to have those streams of light doused by the return of even colder darkness. My bright light before you, Adam walked me out of, what up until that moment, had been my greatest pain, a family who I could not be my family without hurting me, who ultimately rejected me. But nothing could prepare for the loss of him. It was my greatest darkness, even darker than when Crista was taken from me. I was drowning when you found me and would surely have died if you had not. Nick Ruiz, you are the light that brightens my world. You are the one who makes it okay to smile and feel joy. You are the one who I will love above all others in life, and while Adam will always be a part of me, it is you to whom my heart belongs to now. I love you Nick. And I always will. Do me the honor of taking me as your wife, and will do all that I can to honor, cherish, and love you, for the rest of our lives."

The Reverend spoke again.

"The rings?"

"Oh," Kiara laughed, "I almost forgot."

She slid a simple white gold band on to Nick's ring finger inscribed with the words, with much love.

"I do," Nick said smiling.

"The time has come Nick, to speak your heart and bare your soul to your bride as she has done for you. Take her hand in yours and let her know just how much you love her."

Nick smiled down at her and saw in her eyes that she truly loved him above all others. And that she always would. It made what he wanted to say that much easier. Kissing the top of her hand, he spoke with such tenderness and grace he could see the light glowing from within her and it made his heart fill to full capacity with the kind of want to be the better man that only she could inspire him to be.

"My bonita. My angel. My sweet, tough, Kiara. When we met your grief was so powerful, so raw, and so consuming, I had never seen anything like it. I, who had just watched my own life fall apart could not imagine how any one person could love another that much. But on the day we met, I was drowning too, and your pain made mine pale, and your pain seemed so much more visceral than mine that it made me forget, if only for a short time in the beginning that I had lost anything at all. And when my own pain began to set in, you arrived like an angel sent from above. You made me believe I could be the better man, for that you deserve my heart, but the reality is, you had it from the moment I saw you in the chapel mourning the loss of a man I could never be. I am lucky that you accept me into your heart at all. You ask me to do you the honor of taking you as my wife when the reality is it is me who should be asking you to do me the honor of taking me as your husband. I love you Kiara Matthews. And if you'll say I do to taking me as your husband, I promise to love you as I've loved no other for the rest of our lives."

"I do, Nick. Now, put the ring on my finger," she said laughing through joyous tears.

"I inscribed the ring, bonita."

"Copycat."

The small congregation chuckled.

"I inscribed it so that Adam would always be close to your heart while leaving room for me. I inscribed it with the words Number One."

Tears filled her eyes yet again as he slid the ring on her finger.

"Damn it Nick, you're making me cry."

"Good. Because you've already taken my breath away enough to make me cry a hundred times over."

The Reverend Richardson smiled and announced, "You may kiss the bride."

Nick swept her up in his arms, dipped her and laid one of the most sizzling hot kisses on her that she'd yet to experience, even with him. He whispered in her ear as he brought her back to her feet.

"You just wait until after little Crista is born, because there is much, much, more where that came from."

Kiara's heart filled to bursting with joy. She was with a man who would make her happy. No, he wasn't Adam Paul Matthews, but no man could ever be that, Nick Ruiz was a man of passion, a man Adam had sent to her to move on with. That she believed to the depth of her soul. That made it easy to love Nick. To be in love with Nick. To give her life to the man. She wasn't settling, she was building a different sort of life with the man who had made life worth living again. She could only hope to do them proud in the coming years.

Chapter Nineteen

She was so pregnant she couldn't stand it. Kiara lumbered

around her and Nick's large home and cursed the size of it and the fact their bedroom was on the second floor. But a thrill went through her for two reasons. First, she was two weeks over her due date. Little Crista would be arriving any day now. She just wished Adam would help push the little peanut out of her body so she could get to enjoying sex, and sleeping on her side and stomach again.

Second, she could focus her full attention on the tournament run coming up. The Wildcats had managed to exceed the experts expectations and landed a number three seed. Nick didn't want her to go. He thought she was too close to delivery. But she insisted on going. She only had three passions in life. Little Crista, Nick, and UK basketball, she would not be denied. Besides, she got every last coach, and every last player-including Jason Dexter, especially Jason Dexter-to agree to taking a bus to their first and second round games in Chicago, so that she could keep working, and stay close to her husband, in case she went into labor early.

"Come on Kiara, bus is pulling out in an hour."

"Keep your boots on, that bus isn't going anywhere without

us."

"Need I remind you Mitch is still iffy about you working so late into your pregnancy?"

She met Nick in their bedroom, and came up behind him and ran her hands up his chest, while showering his back with slow, sweet kisses. He groaned and turned around, grinning down at her.

"You drive me crazy sometimes."

"I do, do I?"

Holding her face in his hands he kissed.

"I can't wait until we can be together again."

Her face brightened.

"I'd hope so. You married me didn't you."

"I married Rhiannon too, but I didn't feel this way with her."

"So you liked my curves when we met did ya'?"

"When I first met you I was drawn to everything about you. You were this beautiful, ethereal, gorgeous, grief stricken angel sent to me from a man who had loved you so much he died for you. I was lucky to be where I was when I was. And you are still this beautiful, ethereal, gorgeous, angel. But you've heard me tell you this all before. And we've got to go."

"Okay, okay. I just like to hear you say it. Makes me feel good."

He smiled.

"Just wait until after Crista is born. I'll have all kinds of other things to say about you too."

"Like what?"

"Ah, bonita, you'll have to wait to hear those."

"No fair."

"Hey, who knows, you might hear them before this trip is over."

She lit up like the beginning of an early morning sunrise. He caressed her cheek and she leaned into it, closing her eyes. How did he get so damn lucky?

***

The bus ride was bumpy and uncomfortable to say the least. But Kiara refused to complain. She didn't want Nick to know the kind of special physical hell she was going through. As they drove through Illinois she thought of Crista, her best friend of ten years and what they had shared over ten years. Of how they had scrounged up the money to make the trip to see Duke and UK play. Even though Crista had not been dying there had been a sense of this could not last forever hanging over them. Although, neither she nor Crista could have dreamed the nightmarish end Junior would visit upon them. Leaving Kiara, empty, sad, bitter, and terrified to go anywhere except the cemetery, and until recently Junior had taken that away from her too. Even though she'd had to take Nick with her to summon up the courage she'd visited both Adam's and Crista's graves. Closing her eyes she breathed deep and took herself back there to take her mind off the physical agony she was in.

It had been a gray day. Flurries floated down from the sky, and the ground was frozen and hard. As she stood at Crista's headstone she laid a red rose at it, knowing full well that either the groundskeeper or one of Crista's family members would come and remove it. They always did. So dutifully, when she came again, she brought another white rose. Not the cheap kind either the kind that came from Nantz and Kraft's and cost a pretty penny.

Crista had loved white roses. Wherever she was, Kiara

suspected her friend still did.

"You wouldn't believe where I'm going today. Or what I've been up to over the last year. Well, maybe you do. I'm having a baby. I'm married. I've fallen in love. Twice. And I get to scout UK ball games on film. I even get to sit on the bench during the actual game. Can you believe it?" A few tears slid down her cheeks. "I miss you. What happened to you should never have happened. But I got him. I got up the nerve and I got him." Kiara wiped her face off. "Thanks for sending me Adam. If he's up there would you make sure that he's okay? That he's not sad or angry or lonely? He really means a lot to me. This is our baby, and he still has a little piece of my heart, you know? Well, I just wanted to say hello before we headed to Chicago, I've got to go say hi to Adam now. I'll see you again soon."

With Crista there had always been such a sense of guilt. A plaguing madness that she was to blame for what Junior had done. But as she touched the headstone before moving on, a great sense of peace washed over her and she felt the pain washed away as tears streamed down her face. Crista never judged her. And would never have blamed her for what her bastard of an uncle did. It was time she forgave herself. And through the strength of her baby, Adam's love, and the life Nick was blessing her with, she found it was okay to find that place within that allowed her to do just that.

The bus pulled in under the hotel awning and stopped. God she was miserable. She should have laid off the kung po chicken the night before, she had some serious indigestion going on. She thought of Adam and grinned, he would have found this funny. Nick stood up and faced the coaches and the players and smiled.

"Alright everybody. Play our best and win. Because if we don't play our best we're going home after tomorrow. And we will be going home. And tell me, who wants to make a long bus ride home after going out in the first round?"

Complete silence greeted her ears.

"That's the number one rule."

"If Number One looks like she's about to have the baby nothing else matters."

Everybody laughed, except her. Not that she didn't find it funny. But at that moment a cramp seized her body so hard it took her breath away.

"Nick," she said her voice rising.

He turned and faced her. She stood up and the sound of water and amniotic fluid splashing to the ground reverberated throughout the whole bus.

"Coach," the whole bus sang in unison.

"Clyde, Ori," Nick ordered, "get an ambulance. Boys, help me get her off the bus."

Jason came through, and Nick put one of her arms around his neck. Jason did the same on her other side.

"I guess Crista's coming now whether I want her to wait or not."

Nick beamed.

"Angel, she's already so much like you it's unbelievable."

"Well, whatever she's like, she wants out and she wants out now."

"I know."

"If you need to be at practice with the boys I understand," another monster contraction hit her as she sucked the air through her teeth.

"I think Cameron and Clyde can handle it until the baby gets here."

"Nick."

"Yeah."

"Would you call Helen and Michael?"

"I'll do it once we're on our way to the hospital. Okay?"

She nodded and bit down on her lip.

"It's going to be okay, bonita. I'm here."

"And Adam? Do you think he's here too?"

"I'm sure of it, angel, I'm sure of it."

***

"C'mon, you can do this, you can do this. Just do what the doctor says. Push, bonita, push."

She was tired. Too tired. Who was she kidding? She couldn't birth a child. Little Crista didn't feel like such a little Crista, she felt like a bowling bowl trying to squeeze itself out of a whole the size of a small lemon. When she'd gotten to the hospital, they'd told her it was too late for an epidural. So she'd endured five of the longest hours of her life, praying that the baby would just do them all a favor and arrive. Up until then she'd been breathing like she was supposed to, she trying to do it on her own. Then a wave of pain hit her that was so strong she retched. She started to cry.

The doctor smiled.

"One more push. One last hard push."

Nick held his hand out and she looked up at him. This was it. This was the moment she'd been waiting for. For seven months she'd dreamt of what it would be like to hold her child in her arms. Adam's child. As she gazed up into Nick's face she saw the same thing there that she'd seen on Adam's face a year ago. He wanted her. He wanted to be a father. Little Crista's father. Nick kissed her at her temple, she took his hand and pushed as hard as she could.

"That's it, that's it," the doctor coaxed her. Then the sound of her baby girl crying filled her ears, and if she hadn't been crying before, she certainly was now.

They laid the baby at her chest and Nick's eyes glistened with tears as well.

"She's beautiful."

Crista was beautiful. But not because of the way she looked, but because of the echo of Adam's voice in her own. Kiara gazed up at Nick.

"You have to know something."

He smiled down at her.

"What's that?"

"You are a better man."

"Only because you make me want to be one."

"Sir, do you want to cut the cord?"

"I don't know..."

"Do it Nick, you're the father who she's going to know in the flesh. I can keep the memory of Adam alive. But right now, you cut the cord."

"Only because Adam isn't here to do it."

"Of course."

Nick followed the doctor's instructions. Then as she lay there, exhausted and joyous, she heard his voice, Adam's voice.

I love you, Kiara Matthews. I love our daughter. And no matter what I'll be here for you.

She smiled and looked at Nick then looked to the sky.

I love you Adam. Forever and always. As long as our daughter lives I'll love you. Thank you for sending me Nick. I couldn't have asked for a better man.

www.ingramcontent.com/pod-product-compliance
Lightning Source LLC
Chambersburg PA
CBHW020606260626
47157CB00003B/884